The Amish Helper

Samantha Collier

Published by Trellis Publishing, 2021.

THE AMISH HELPER

First edition. July 16, 2021.

Copyright © 2021 Samantha Collier.

ISBN: 979-8224098019

Written by Samantha Collier.

THE AMISH HELPER

SAMANTHA COLLIER

The Amish Helper

Hope watched as the familiar farmhouse came into view. She hadn't been here in years, but surprisingly, it hadn't changed very much.

"Steady there, Prancer!" Her father's voice, guiding the buggy along the rough dirt track toward the home, pierced her reverie. It was a wet day, and rain was even now pelting the track, making the horses' hooves lose their footing in the ruts.

Hope peered through the rain, carefully assessing the state of the house. In the old days, it had been a dazzling white; lovingly maintained. But now, the paint was peeling, coming off in long strips. The weatherboard railing on the veranda needed repairs. Hope could see that there was a trail of children's toys left haphazardly along it, which were getting wet where holes in the roofing leaked.

She shook her head, a sudden sadness overwhelming her. It shouldn't be like this. But it was, and that was one reason she was here.

Her father drew up the horses, jumping down from the buggy and walking around to help Hope down. The large black umbrella he opened shielded them from the rain as they quickly ran up the front steps. As her father knocked on the door, Hope could hear children running around, their shrieks carrying through the air.

There was no response. Her father knocked again, louder this time. Eventually, they heard a man calling for them to come in.

Her father gave her a rueful smile as he opened the door. They proceeded in, almost colliding with two children who were chasing each other down the hallway.

"It's Annie's turn!" yelled a fair-haired boy, looking over his shoulder. Then he stopped, gazing up at the two people in the hallway.

"I remember you!" he said, staring at Hope. "Aren't you my mamm's cousin?"

Hope smiled. "*Jah*, I am your Mamm's cousin," she said, kneeling so that she was on eye level with the youngster. "My name is Hope. What is yours again?" Hope knew very well what the boy's name was, but she didn't want to overwhelm him.

"Eli," said the boy, shyly. "And Annie's my sister." He pointed at a girl with long golden hair, who had just come into the hallway and was watching them.

Hope straightened, and nodded to Annie. "Well, Eli, can you tell me where your Daed is? My father and I need to see him."

Eli nodded, his large blue eyes assessing them both. "Follow me," he said, walking into the living room.

Hope looked over the room. It was a mess; in addition to toys, there were clothes draped over every surface, and plates and cutlery still on the table. It was obvious that there hadn't been any cleaning done for quite a while.

Then her eyes were drawn to the figure, lying on the sofa. Her breath suddenly stilled, and her heart started to thud uncomfortably. He was the same, wasn't he? Those impossible blue eyes, and the brown hair that glinted with flecks of gold. But his beard was longer, and looked unkempt. He didn't smile.

"You're here," he said, in a monotone. Hope didn't think he sounded pleased.

"Jacob." Hope nodded at him, trying to still her hands, which had started to tremble. Why? Why, after all this time, was this still happening to her?

But Jacob hadn't noticed. He was staring past her to her father, who had followed her into the room.

"Mr Miller." Jacob attempted to straighten himself on the sofa, pulling himself up with difficulty. "I am sorry that I can't stand to greet you."

Hope's father smiled. "Jacob, it is alright," he answered softly. "We understand. It is why we are here, after all."

Jacob sighed. "The doctor says that I need to rest it completely for about a week," he said, pointing to his right leg, which was encased in plaster. "I'm not allowed to do anything, apparently."

"How did it happen?" Mr Miller had perched on the edge of the sofa, staring down at Jacob.

"At the dairy." Jacob's eyes clouded. "One of the cows kicked me, and I lost my footing on the slippery floor. I fell down a level, and landed badly." He grimaced at the memory.

"The pain is bad?" Mr Miller watched his face.

"Very bad, but I can cope." Jacob gazed at him. "It's everything else that is the issue now." He spread his arm wide, to indicate the house, and the children.

Mr Miller nodded. "*Jah*, it is difficult for you," he replied. "But Hope is here, now. She will tend to the children, and the housework."

Jacob's face tightened. "It shouldn't be for long," he said, through gritted teeth. He still hadn't looked at her, not really. Hope felt her heart sink to the floor. Why was he being this way? She was here for him and his children, after all. She didn't expect lashings of gratitude, but a civil manner would be appropriate, wouldn't it?

There was an awkward silence. Mr Miller coughed, putting his black hat back onto his head.

"Yes, well, I should be off," he said, looking at Hope. His eyes were full of sympathy. "Farewell, Jacob. I hope that your recovery is quick."

"Thank you, Mr Miller," Jacob replied.

Hope walked back to the front door with her father. The rain was unrelenting, pelting the house with a ferocity that worried Hope.

"You will be alright, driving back in this?" she said, turning to her father, frowning.

"I will be fine, Hope," the older man answered. "It is you that I am worried about. He doesn't treat you with the respect that you deserve. If you feel that you don't want to be here any longer, let me know, and I will come straight away for you. We can find someone else to help him until he recovers." He frowned. "He is still bitter. The grace of God has not let forgiveness into his heart, and any woman that he encounters must suffer the burden of it."

Hope smiled. "It will be fine, Daed. I am strong! And it is only for a little while, after all."

"You are sure?"

"I am very sure." Hope reached up and gently kissed her father. He was such a wonderful man, always looking out for her. She couldn't have wished for a better father.

"Farewell, then, daughter." He reached down and stroked her arm, then strode out. Hope could see him open the umbrella again, then run to the buggy.

She sighed. The children's screams had reached high pitch again, and she could see Jacob was pretending to sleep on the sofa. He didn't want to talk to her now, obviously.

There was nothing for it. She would just have to roll up her sleeves, and jump in.

***

Hope had just put the children to bed, after a long drawn out battle. They had lingered too long in their baths, saying that they always stayed that long. Then there had been the myriad of excuses as to why they couldn't stay in bed. Annie needed a drink of water. Eli had to go to the toilet, just one more time.

But eventually, they had settled. They had even enjoyed the bedtime story that she had read them – one of her own favourites from childhood.

Walking down the stairs and into the living room, she surveyed the house as she went. It had taken all afternoon, but the house was now spic and span. Three loads of washing had been done, and a mountain of dishes washed. She had even managed to cook a big platter of fried chicken and coleslaw for supper, which the children had woofed down.

Jacob had barely muttered a "*danke*" when she had brought supper into him, on a tray. But she noticed that he had polished it all off, nonetheless.

She hovered, now, at the edge of the living room, looking at him. He was reading a book, and didn't glance at her.

"Ahem." She cleared her throat, and eventually he raised his eyes to hers. "The children are settled. Do you need some help getting to your own room for the night?"

Jacob shook his head quickly. "I will manage," he said. "I have the crutches." His gaze lingered just behind her.

Hope sighed. "Well, I might retire then," she said. "Good night."

He nodded, looking back down to his book. Hope lingered a moment longer, then walked slowly back up the stairs to the guest bedroom where she was staying.

It was a pretty room; the wallpaper was white, embossed with a delicate rose motif, and the curtains were handmade in a similar pattern. Hope walked up to them, gently stroking them. She remembered when Emma had bought the fabric for them, and how excited she had been.

"I am making curtains for my new home!' she had laughed. "I am a married woman, now, Hope! Can you believe it? I must pinch myself sometimes, to believe it myself! Oh, how happy I am!"

Hope smiled ruefully, still stroking the curtains. But the happiness was not destined to last. It was probably one of Gott's blessings, that none of them had known what the future held...

Hope and Emma had been the very best of friends, always. There was only two years age difference, after all, and they had been brought up closely. First cousins.

It had been after rumspringa that Hope had started noticing the handsome young man, who stared at them down the length of the long table during the meal after church service. Jacob King, was his name.

At first, she and Emma had giggled, and thought nothing of it. They had been so close at that stage, and it didn't seem possible that a man could ever come between them, or challenge that bond.

But then Jacob had started approaching them. He was charming. At first, he talked to them both equally. Hope started to become excited when she thought that she might see him, and to take extra care with her appearance.

He liked her, she knew that he did. He would often stare at her, those incredible blue eyes glowing like sapphires.

Looking back, she could never isolate the moment when that had changed. When he had stopped looking at her, and instead focused those eyes on Emma.

It had been subtle, at first. He talked to Emma more than to her. And then, the two of them would walk off together, and not return for a while. Hope tried very hard to act happy for them, but inside, she was crushed. She tried to stop her feelings for Jacob, but they stayed, coiled at the base of her heart.

Jacob and Emma. Courting. And then, suddenly, they were engaged.

Hope had been bridesmaid at their wedding, and still remembered how sore her face had been from smiling. At the first opportunity, she had left. How was she ever going to still be their friend, when she felt this way?

She helped Emma set up her new home. She had shared in the joy of their children being born. But then Emma had started to change, growing restless and distant. Gradually, she stopped seeing Hope altogether. Hope was worried, but didn't see what she could do. And – she could only admit this to herself – she was a bit relieved. It had been hard, pretending all the time that she didn't feel the way that she did about Jacob. Oh, she knew that she had lost, and had accepted that. But it was still hard.

She also missed Emma. They had been so close, once upon a time.

When she had first heard the news, she had felt as if someone had come up to her and punched her in the stomach. She felt winded. Emma had abandoned her husband and children; she had taken off with an Englisher, and left the district completely.

Hope could still feel the shock of it. As she remembered that awful moment, she clutched the curtains tighter.

The whole district had been abuzz with talk of it; it had been the scandal of the decade. But even that wasn't the worst of it, for poor Jacob and his children. For after six months, word had filtered back that Emma had been killed in a car accident. Her *kinder*, already abandoned, had lost their mother forever.

And Jacob had lost the woman who had decided that she no longer wanted to be his wife.

Hope could only imagine the pain of it. He had withdrawn from the community, looking after his children and managing his dairy farm alone. He had spurned all offers of assistance. He had seemed to want to hibernate like a wounded bear in a cave, guarding his cubs ferociously.

That was until he had broken his leg. And Hope had answered the call to duty, no matter what personal pain it cost her.

She studied the curtains closely, running her finger over the pattern, as if the meaning of it all might suddenly be revealed in the fabric. He didn't want her here, that was obvious. He was as cold and distant as if she were a stranger. She had not seen him in many years, but they had once been friends...could he not put the past behind him, just a little, and remember that?

Hope sighed, dropping the curtains abruptly. It didn't matter. She had a duty to do, and the main part of that was making sure that Eli and Annie were properly cared for and the house tended, until their father was back on his feet.

She simply had to close her mind to everything else.

***

"Annie! Give it back to me!"

Eli reached across the table, lunging forward. He was attempting to grab a book of his that Annie had picked up. The little girl laughed, picking up the book and holding it above her head.

"Children!" Hope put on her stern voice. "We are respectful at the breakfast table." She drew a deep breath. "Annie, please put the book down. You haven't finished your muffin. Eli, pick up your fork and start eating your scrapple, please."

The children grumbled, but did what they were told.

Lying on the sofa, where he had been since he had gotten out of bed, Jacob King listened to the squabbling, smiling grimly to himself. Hope had her work cut out for her with those two. He didn't know if his late wife's cousin really understood the hard work involved in running a house and looking after children.

Jacob raised himself, so that he was propped higher on the cushions behind him, causing his injured leg to fall slightly. He winced at the sudden stab of pain, crying out.

Hope rushed into the room, concern knotting her brow. "Are you alright, Jacob?"

He waved his hand at her dismissively. "Just moving," he replied, in an irritated voice. Hope watched him for a moment, before she shrugged her shoulders and went back to the breakfast table.

Jacob looked down, ashamed of himself. He knew that he was being unbearably rude to her, but he couldn't seem to stop himself. Just seeing a woman – any woman – in the house again, tending chores and looking after the children, caused him such anguish it was all that he could do not to order her to pack her bags immediately.

But this wasn't just any woman. This was Hope, who had been his wife's cousin and best friend. Back when they were courting, and first married. Before his wife had inexplicably changed.

Jacob frowned, remembering. A sudden vision of Hope, as she had been when he first met her, entered his mind. He had not thought about it in years, but it had been Hope who had first sparked his interest. But then Emma, with all her sparkle and charm, had caught his eye. And the rest was history.

Very bad history, as it turned out. Emma had never been suited to marriage and motherhood. He should have seen the signs earlier – she had always been restless and flighty, flitting from one thing to the next, never able to concentrate for long. He had thought that marriage would calm her, but if anything, it had magnified it.

Abandonment. And then, death. Gone forever, now.

Jacob's heart filled with sorrow, quickly supplanted by anger. He could hear Hope in the kitchen, singing softly to herself while she did the breakfast dishes. The sound of her sweet voice caused such distress in him, he spoke before he could think any further.

"I need to rest!" he called out.

Hope stopped singing.

Jacob had gotten what he wanted. Why, then, did he suddenly feel so bereft, as if he would do anything for her to ignore him, and start singing again?

***

Hope had just collected the eggs from the henhouse. She turned to Eli and Annie.

"The girls have supplied so many eggs today," she said, smiling. "Would you like to bake a cake?"

They nodded eagerly, their eyes shining.

"Now," she said, looking around the kitchen, "I need some help. Eli, can you get out a big mixing bowl and wooden spoon. Annie, can you open the pantry and bring me some flour, butter and sugar."

The children set to work. Hope smiled to herself. Should she just automatically bake a cake that she knew by heart, or should she involve them further, and find a different recipe?

She glanced around the kitchen. There were some high shelves in the corner, where a few old dusty books lived. She walked over and reached up, grabbing one and pulling it down.

Amish Baking Made Easy. Hope recognised it as a wedding gift to Emma and Jacob. It had been a bit of a joke between them all. "Are people suggesting that I can't cook?" Emma had said. Jacob had smiled, knowing it was true. Hope had diplomatically said that everyone could do with some new recipes. But it was true – Emma was a hopeless cook, despite having helped her own mother since she was little.

"What's that?" Eli's voice behind her made her jump.

Hope blew some dust from the cover. "Just an old recipe book," she said. "I thought that maybe we could find a good recipe in here for a wonderful cake!"

Eli peered at it intently. "Was it my mother's?" He stared at her solemnly, his blue eyes large in his face.

Hope's heart constricted, but she steadied her voice. *"Jah,"* she replied, not looking at him. "Have a look through it, Eli, and pick a recipe."

Eli opened the book, poring over the pages. Annie stopped what she was doing, and came and looked through it with him.

Such a simple scene. Two siblings looking through a cookbook. But Hope's heart lurched, again, thinking of her cousin, and how it should be her here, doing this with her children. Why had Emma abandoned them? And how could she have done it?

Hope shook her head. She would never know. Emma had gone to her grave with her secrets.

"What about a ginger cake, Hope?" Eli stopped turning the pages, looking up at her.

Hope walked over, peering at the recipe over his shoulder. "*Jah*, we could do that," she smiled. "I think we have all of the ingredients."

The two children smiled at her, eagerly.

***

The smell of ginger cake baking was making Jacob's mouth water. He had forgotten how wonderful the smell of fresh baking was; it had been so long. The smell seemed to spread through the house, wafting into all the rooms.

Hope was obviously a great cook. The fried chicken last night was just about the best that he had ever tasted, and her scrapple this morning for breakfast had been wonderful, as well.

He could barely wait to sample the ginger cake. There were advantages to having a woman in the house...and not just any woman. Hope had managed – in the space of one afternoon and one morning – to completely clean the house and outside, cook magnificently, deal with loads of washing and amuse his children. All with a smile on her face.

And all while he was being rude to her. Jacob felt a stab of guilt.

He watched her as she walked from the kitchen with the cake. Eli followed her, balancing plates, a cutting knife, and forks. Annie brought up the rear, holding a small pitcher of cream.

"Shall we?" Hope took the knife, cutting into the cake. The two children's eyes glowed as they watched.

She walked into the living room to Jacob, carrying a plate with a big slice of ginger cake and a dollop of cream on the side.

"The children made it themselves," she smiled. "I just helped!"

"*Danke.*" Jacob held out his hand. As she passed it to him, their hands touched, causing a jolt of electricity to course through him. He looked at Hope, shocked.

She had obviously felt it, too, judging by the way she pulled her hand back as if it had been burnt.

"Well..." she said. She refused to look him in the eye. "Enjoy."

She turned and quickly walked back to the kitchen.

What had just happened? His hand felt like it had been electrocuted. But then the smell of the cake wafted up, and he couldn't resist. He dug his fork in, and took a large mouthful.

It was divine, of course. He knew that they had gotten the recipe from an old cookbook of Emma's; he had heard them talking in the kitchen. He even remembered when Emma had attempted to make this very cake, once upon a time.

It hadn't turned out like this. This was one of the best cakes that he had ever eaten.

He watched Hope, sitting at the kitchen table next to his children. They were all eating their own slices with relish. Now and again, the children would ask Hope a question, which she would answer patiently and with humour.

Eli and Annie obviously adored her, already. But then, how could they not? Hope really *was* wonderful. And it had been a long time since any woman had been in this house, and cared for them.

Jacob felt a surge of anger nudge the tender feeling aside. He didn't want a woman in here! Women spoilt everything. He had been managing quite well, as a single father....at least until he had broken his leg.

He nodded his head, decisively. It didn't matter how delectable a cook she was, or how loving and patient with his children. He tried to forget her sweetness, and the magic he had felt when their hands had touched.

He wanted her gone. How long until his silly leg healed, and he and his children could go back to life as it was?

***

A week had flown past, and it was almost time for Hope to leave.

She felt very conflicted. She had grown to love Eli and Annie, and it had been wonderful being so independent, running a house. On days when it had been raining, she and Annie had quilted together, or they had all baked again. And when the weather had been fine, they had worked outside. Tending the large vegetable garden, and gathering the eggs. Sometimes, they had walked further, over the hill, collecting wildflowers as they walked.

She was going to miss them. Even thinking about it brought tears to her eyes.

But Jacob had gone to the doctor yesterday, who had told him that the cast could come off soon. He would still need crutches, of course, but he would be able to manage. She wasn't going to be needed anymore.

Jacob. She shook her head as she thought of him. He was such a paradox! Sometimes, she had caught him looking at her almost tenderly. At those times, he would talk softly and gently to her, and she remembered the man she had fallen in love with, all those years ago. He was still there! You had to scratch the surface a bit, but he was!

But then, the other Jacob would suddenly re-surface. The bitter man, who couldn't put the past behind him, and wanted to lash out at everyone around him. Hope understood why he did it, but it didn't make it any easier to bear. Especially when she was here to help, and especially when she felt the way that she did about him.

She loved him. She probably always would. It seemed to be her cross to bear, in life.

Hope stared around the kitchen, which was sparkling. She had made it sparkle; she had gotten down on her knees and scrubbed every inch of it. She had even changed a few things around, to make it easier for her. Just little things – the bowls into a cupboard that was easier for her to reach; fresh herbs picked from the garden in small pots on a ledge, the better to pick quickly when she was cooking.

It made her realise how much she craved her own home – and her own children. She was twenty-eight years old, after all. A confirmed spinster in the district. Destined to live forever in her parents' home, because she would never marry. How could she? The only man that she had ever loved was Jacob.

There had been a few marriage proposals, over the years, but she had turned them all down. A marriage without love was not a marriage, in Hope's opinion. It was as simple as that.

But the yearning had been re-awakened, staying here. Looking after Eli and Annie. Such beautiful children, who needed a mother's love. Oh, she had no doubt that Jacob coped as well as he could, but it wasn't the same, was it? Hope remembered the state of the house when she had first come to stay. As hard as Jacob tried, he would never be able to keep on top of everything. He had to work in the dairy, after all.

"Are you alright, Hope?"

She turned around, to see Annie standing there. Her big blue eyes looked concerned.

Hope smiled. "Of course I am, Annie. I was just thinking how much I will miss you all, when it is time for me to go."

"You aren't leaving us, are you?" The little girl's eyes widened in distress. "Hope, please don't go!"

Hope crouched down so that she was on eye level with the girl. "I was only ever staying until your Daed's leg got better, Annie. I thought that you knew that."

"*Jah*, but..." the little girl's voice trailed off, and her eyes filled with tears. "Who will bake cakes with us? And take us for walks? Daed is always too busy to do those things."

Hope's heart felt like it was breaking into a million pieces. "I will come over again, I promise! We can do things together. I am sorry that I haven't been around much." And that was very true. She should have soldiered through her heartbreak over Jacob, and been here for these children. They needed someone, that was obvious.

There was a sound at the doorway. They both looked around, to see Jacob standing there, leaning against the doorframe. His crutches were by his side.

"You are leaving us soon, then?" He looked at Hope, his eyes probing hers.

Hope took a deep breath. "Well, you are almost better," she said, not looking at him. "You don't need me anymore, do you?"

He continued to gaze at her. He seemed like he was about to say something else, but then he shook his head slightly, and turned and left the kitchen.

***

Hope walked through the back door of her home, crying out when she saw her mother.

"Mamm!" She threw her arms around the older woman, hugging her tightly.

Mrs Miller gazed at her daughter, lovingly. "My Hope," she said, her eyes shining. "I have missed you, my *lieb*."

"I have missed you too, Mamm," said Hope, taking off her bonnet and cape and hanging them on the hook in the corner. "How has everyone been?"

"Well," replied her mother. "Sit down at the table, Hope. I have just brewed a fresh pot of coffee, and I have some leftover apple strudel we can have for morning tea."

Hope did as she was told, carefully pouring the coffee for both her mother and herself. Her mother cut generous slices of the strudel.

"How were things at the Kings?" her mother asked, after they had both taken the first sip of black coffee and a bite of the strudel.

"As well as they can be," replied Hope, carefully. "Jacob is much improved. I organised things where I could, to make it easier for him." She took a deep breath. "Eli and Annie are wonderful! I am going to miss them."

"It would be very hard for them, without their mother," Mrs Miller said. "I have always felt very sorry for them, and wondered why Jacob has been the way that he has. So many in the community have offered to help him with them, but he spurns everyone."

"I think it is his bitterness," said Hope, taking another sip of coffee. "He does dwell in it, Mamm. I think he is distrustful of all women, because of what happened with Emma."

"Emma was always flighty," replied Mrs Miller, darkly. "The grass was always greener on the other side for that girl. I was distressed when she abandoned her family, but deep down, I wasn't surprised. I always saw it in her."

Hope looked at her mother in shock. She had never said so before, at least not to her. "I thought that you liked Emma, Mamm!"

Mrs Miller pursed her lips. "I liked her well enough, mainly because you and she were so close. But I never trusted her. People always act according to their true nature."

Hope took another bite of her strudel, thinking. It was true – Emma had always been capricious. But Hope had made allowances for it, because she had loved her. In the end, it had not been possible.

"Did Jacob express appreciation for your help?" Mrs Miller asked, breaking through Hope's thoughts.

Hope smiled, but it didn't reach her eyes. "I don't think it is possible for him to express gratitude," she replied. "Sometimes, I can see the old Jacob there..." she drifted off, staring into space.

Mrs Miller put her hand over Hope's on the table. "You have always loved him, haven't you, Hope?"

Hope's eyes widened, and then filled with tears. "I thought that I hid it so well," she whispered.

Mrs Miller's eyes were shining with tears, too. "You did hide it well, Hope. I doubt that anyone but me would have suspected. I saw how excited you would get when you would speak to him, and then how that excitement faded once it became obvious that he and Emma were an item. A mother knows, my dear."

"Well, it was never meant to be," Hope replied. She looked down at their joined hands. "I have gotten over it."

"Have you?" Her mother looked at her, sharply.

Hope looked up at her mother, laughing. "Of course I have, Mamm!" she said.

Mrs Miller gazed at her daughter, in sorrow. She knew that Hope still loved Jacob. Why couldn't the silly man see what a treasure she was? Why was he so mired in the past that he couldn't see anything for the future?

Emma was gone. It was a tragedy, but it had happened. Jacob needed to move into the future, not just for his sake, but for his children's.

And for Hope's.

***

"Could you pass the mop, please, Hope?"

Mrs Miller and her daughter were spring cleaning the attic, and were covered in dust and cobwebs. Hope sneezed. She reached out to the mop and passed it to her mother, rolling her eyes.

"Spring cleaning is my least favourite job in the world," Hope said.

"At least it only comes around once a year," her mother replied, wiping a cobweb from her face.

Suddenly, they heard a loud knock at the front door. They both looked at each other, questioningly. No, there were no visitors expected.

"Hope, would you?" her mother asked. "You are closer to the door than me."

"Of course, Mamm," she replied, walking down the narrow stairwell. There was another knock, louder this time.

Hope ran toward it, reefing it open.

It was Jacob King. He stood leaning against the doorframe, crutches in one hand. In the other, he had a freshly picked bouquet of wildflowers.

Hope's heart lurched, then started thudding painfully within her breast. "Jacob," she whispered. "What are you doing here?"

"Can I come in?"

"Of course." Hope automatically let him enter. She couldn't think clearly; she felt as if her mind was clouded. "Come into the kitchen. I will make us some coffee."

He followed her into the kitchen, barely using his crutches.

"So, you are all improved?" Hope asked, as she started brewing the coffee. What was he doing here?

"Much better, thank you." He gazed at her. Then he abruptly thrust the bouquet at her. "These are for you."

Hope took them. "Thank you," she whispered. She didn't understand. Why was Jacob giving her flowers? Was this a belated attempt at gratitude, for her coming to stay and helping him?

"Hope."

She turned around, for where she was trying to find a vase. "*Jah*?" she whispered.

"I need to talk to you." Jacob took a deep breath. "I know that you will probably tell me that I am a stupid fool, but I can't contain it any longer." He took another deep breath. "I haven't been able to stop thinking about you, since you left us. I know that I was terribly rude to you, when you were staying, and I am so sorry."

"Jacob, it's alright..."

"No, let me finish." He gazed at her, his eyes filled with tears. "Hope, you have no idea how hard it was, seeing another woman in the kitchen, and tending the children! It brought up all my issues over Emma. It was wrong; I shouldn't have taken it out on you."

"I understand..."

"No, you don't, Hope." His voice had started to shake. "It wasn't just that. I started to enjoy you being there, and realised what a wonderful person you are. But I was trying to fight it, telling myself that I didn't want another woman in my life – ever! But I can't fight it anymore, Hope. I find that I love you."

Hope gasped. "You love me?"

He nodded, staring at her. "I love you, with all of my heart. I am still scared, I can't deny it. But I needed to try. If you have no interest in me, please tell me know." He hung his head.

Hope's heart lifted. "Oh, Jacob! If you only knew! I love you, too. I have loved you forever."

Jacob's eyes widened. "You have always loved me? Oh, Hope! If only I had have known! I was very interested in you, when we first met, but then Emma took over..."

"It was as it should be," replied Hope, her voice tremulous. "It was all a part of Gott's plan. Eli and Annie wouldn't be here, if you both hadn't fallen in love and married." She took a deep breath. "I know that it is still hard, Jacob, but you have to look at what was good, as well as what was bad. Yes, Emma abandoned you all, and then she died. But she gave you the children."

Jacob's eyes glittered with tears. "It is so true, Hope, my *lieb*. You are so wise! I would be so happy if you would do me the honour of becoming my wife, and the new mother to my children."

Hope felt like she was in a dream. Could it really be happening? All her dreams were suddenly coming true.

She turned to him, looking him in the eye. "Nothing would give me more pleasure, Jacob."

They smiled at each other. Perhaps the past had finally been laid to rest, once and for all.

THE END

STARTING OVER

21

STEPHANIE SWIFT

Veronica Lansing didn't know whether she was coming or going. Glancing at the clock on the wall behind her, she winced when she saw it was only noon. Five more hours to go until quitting time.

"Veronica? Did you hear me?"

Her line of vision was suddenly obscured by a clipboard and stark-white medical forms. Putting a finger on top of them, she pushed down so she could look over them, only to find her friend and coworker, Joanie, grinning at her.

"I really hope you're wanting my autograph, because if I see another patient release form I have to type in this computer, I'm going to scream," Veronica said.

Joanie put the forms on top of the counter and leaned over to look at her more closely. When she pouted her lips, Veronica rolled her eyes and continued typing information into the computer.

"Pouting won't work either," she remarked.

Joanie laughed.

"Someone's being a grouch today. Did you not have your Double Ristretto Venti Half-Soy Nonfat Decaf Organic Chocolate Brownie Iced Vanilla Double-Shot Gingerbread Extra Hot with Foam Whipped Cream Upside Down Double Blended Frappuccino this morning?"

Veronica rolled her eyes heavenward again.

"You are so funny," she said. "You know I don't ask for the whipped cream."

Joanie giggled one more time as she walked around the nurses station desk and plopped down on the chair beside her. When she placed the forms on the desk and slid them in her direction, she kept her eyes on the computer screen.

"Okay, all joking aside," Joanie said. "I'm going to lunch, and I have a patient in recovery room three. Mid-30's. Rotator cuff surgery. He should be waking up from the anesthesia any minute now. Oh, and did I mention he's cute too?"

Veronica gave up. There was no way she was ever going to get caught up on her paperwork. After saving the file in her computer, she turned off the monitor and looked at Joanie, who was now grinning like a Cheshire cat.

"Cute, huh? Well, you can have him. I'm spoken for," she replied with a wink.

Joanie opened one of the desk drawers and retrieved her purse.

"Ah, yes. The handsome and dashing Dr. Prescott. How could I forget?"

Veronica let her thoughts wander. How could anyone forget Phil Prescott? He was, after all, the best-looking doctor in the whole clinic. She sighed happily when she pictured him in her mind – tall, jet-black hair, dreamy blue eyes – not to mention the most important part... he was a DOCTOR.

"While you sit there and daydream, I'll be in the cafeteria finding something to eat. I'll be back in an hour. Don't forget...recovery room three!"

When Joanie jumped up from her seat, Veronica groaned as she watched her take one bouncy step after another down the empty corridor. It just wasn't normal. People weren't supposed to be that chipper so early in the day. Were they?

Veronica grabbed the forms and began making her way toward recovery room three. Thankfully, they had only two surgeries scheduled for the afternoon, so she might be lucky enough to get caught up on her paperwork. Phil was set to perform one of the more complicated surgeries, so that would be a bright spot to her day. At least she would be able to see him, for a few minutes anyway.

When her father hired him to work at his outpatient surgery clinic after Phil moved to Atlanta two years prior, she never would have guessed he would ask her out. He was one of the most sought-after surgeons in the state, but unfortunately that title also came with his fair share of "groupies" too. Women, especially those in the medical profession, were always fawning over him, which was disheartening as much as it was irritating.

Veronica glanced down at the forms and her feet came to an abrupt halt when she saw the patient's name. Wyatt McDevitt. Now that was a name that hadn't crossed her mind in a very long time.

She shook her head. *No, it couldn't possibly be the same person.*

Yet, when she opened the door to room three and pulled back the curtain surrounding the bed, her heart fluttered when she discovered it was very much Wyatt McDevitt, her ex-boyfriend from high school. Thankfully, he was still sleeping, since she didn't trust herself to speak, and the lump that suddenly lodged in her throat didn't help matters either.

He looked the same except for a few gray tendrils in his wavy brown hair and a little bit of facial hair. It was odd, since she was so used to seeing him clean-shaven, but the scruffiness worked to give him an older and wiser appearance. And, yes, she had to admit he was undeniably just as handsome as she remembered him. She noticed on his forms that he'd marked "single" by relationship status, and for some annoying reason that made her smile a lot more than it should have.

When he started moving around, Veronica tore her eyes away from the forms so she could focus. *Alright, Veronica, stop being nosey and do your job. He's no different than any other patient here.* She silently reprimanded herself for being so caught up in seeing him again that she forgot where she was, and not to mention the circumstances that led to their break up in the first place.

"Roni?"

Her heart did another flip when the familiar deep sound of his voice filled the space around her. No one else, besides her parents, had ever called her by her nickname – not even Phil. She smiled as she placed the forms on a table nearby and elevated the head of the bed to make him more comfortable.

"Hey, stranger," she replied. "How are you feeling?"

He grinned.

"Is it really you?" he asked.

Veronica fluffed the pillow behind his head, mainly just to distract herself more than anything else. She felt tongue-tied. He seemed genuinely happy to see her, but she reminded herself that he was probably still loopy from the anesthesia, and she knew not to take anything he did or said at face value, at least not until it wore off.

"Yes, it's really me. Can I get you anything? Is there someone in the waiting room I can call for you?"

He had such an endearing goofy grin. Unable to stop herself, she smiled back at him, and when he reached out and grasped her wrist, her heart started racing.

"It's so good to see you," he said. "I'm sorry I didn't have time to make myself more presentable."

He looked down at his hospital gown and laughed. Oh yes, he was definitely still loopy from the anesthesia. He slurred his words, and his hazel eyes were glazed over from the medication. She hoped he might go back to sleep, but he continued holding her arm and she didn't have the heart to try and pull away. He rubbed his thumb against her skin, and the softness of it made her swallow hard.

Okay, any minute now and the drugs will knock him out again.

"You know...I never stopped loving you," he mumbled.

Veronica sucked in a breath, but she knew he was coming off the anesthesia and probably had no idea what he was saying. At that time, one of the other nurses walked by the door, and she called out to get her attention.

"Amy, would you please go to the waiting room and see if Mr. McDevitt has anyone here with him?"

Amy nodded and left, but Wyatt never said another word. The way he stared at her made her feel uncomfortable because she knew that look all too well from the time they were together. It was the same lovesick, forlorn expression he often gave her when they were teenagers.

If he hadn't been so drugged, she probably would've thought it was adorable.

A few seconds later an elderly man and woman entered the room with Amy. When the woman went to hug Wyatt, he finally released her wrist and Veronica took the opportunity to move to the end of the bed and out of arm's-length from him.

"How did the surgery go? Were there any complications?" the man asked.

Veronica picked up the forms and looked through them to see if the surgeon had posted any comments or instructions.

"I don't see anything written here, so it must have gone smoothly. He's still coming off the anesthesia, so he'll doze off and on for a little while longer. You can stay here with him, if you like."

She glanced at Wyatt, who had closed his eyes and drifted back to la-la-land. The woman nodded as she gently patted his arm.

"Yes, dear, we'd like to stay, if that's alright. We're the only family he has here, and we hate for him to be alone when he wakes up."

Veronica thought briefly about Wyatt's parents, who divorced when he was twelve, and she wondered for a moment where they were or if something might have happened to them. She wanted to ask, but that would begin a long discussion over how she knew him, and she honestly didn't want to get that conversation started...with anyone.

"Wyatt works as a youth pastor at my church in Conway. I'm Bro. Troy Davidson. This is my wife, Elizabeth."

As she shook their outstretched hands, Veronica wanted to laugh out loud, but she held it inside. Wyatt McDevitt, a youth pastor? No, that couldn't possibly be right. She looked at him, recalling the many times he'd gotten into trouble when he was a teenager and how she'd been his willing accomplice far too many times than she cared to remember. After-school detention was his home away from home, and if there was trouble to be had, Wyatt could sniff it out better than anyone.

"It's nice meeting you," she replied. "I'll let you have some privacy, but I'll be right down the hall at the nurse's station if you need me. When he wakes up he'll stay in recovery for at least another hour, just to make sure he doesn't have any complications from the surgery or anesthesia, before we let him go home."

Bro. Davidson gave her a warm smile.

"Thank you so much," he said.

Veronica nodded slowly as she backed away from his bed. When she pulled the curtain closed around them, she stood there for a moment to gather her thoughts. Wyatt McDevitt was working as a youth pastor. Now there was an outcome she never would have dreamed possible. Perhaps miracles did exist after all.

* * * *

Wyatt sat on the edge of the hospital bed and tried to collect his bearings while waiting for Bro. Troy and Mrs. Elizabeth to return for him. His shoulder wasn't hurting, but he knew it wouldn't be long before the pain medication wore off, and he hoped he would be home by then. He couldn't remember much since waking up from the operation, but he could very vividly recall Roni Lansing being there.

Wyatt closed his eyes and groaned. After all these long years, and he finally sees her while he's drugged and wearing a flimsy hospital gown. It wasn't the good impression he hoped to make when and if he ever saw her again. Wyatt pressed the emergency call button on his hospital bed remote and whispered a prayer that Roni was still somewhere in the vicinity.

"Wyatt? Can I come in?"

He smiled when he heard her voice a few seconds later, and after announcing she could enter, she slowly pulled the curtain aside and stepped inside. Twenty-three years apart, and she was still just as beautiful as he remembered. Her shoulder-length brown hair was pulled away from her face and tied loosely at the nape of her neck, and when she moved closer he could smell the familiar vanilla scent of her perfume.

"How are you feeling?" she asked. "Are you hurting?"

Wyatt sat up straight as she carefully adjusted the strap on his sling. He tried not to watch her every move, but it was difficult not to. He'd spent many nights dreaming of being this close to her again, and he felt the urgent need to soak in every second in case she suddenly disappeared like she had before.

"I feel fine. I just wanted to see you."

Her cheeks flushed a sweet shade of red, and she glanced at him for a split second before taking a step back.

"It's been a long time," she said.

Wyatt nodded. It had been far too long. He wanted to speak freely, to tell her how his life had changed since their breakup, but he felt rushed for time, knowing that Bro. Troy and Mrs. Elizabeth would be returning for him any minute.

"How have you been?" he asked. "How is your family?"

She started walking back and forth around the room, straightening up medical supplies, pressing buttons on machines, and gathering garbage to throw away, as if his questioning made her uncomfortable.

"We've been doing great. My dad owns this clinic, and I've worked here since I graduated from nursing school. A couple of years ago, my mom retired from teaching. Mr. Davidson mentioned that you're a youth pastor at his church."

He furrowed a brow. He didn't know the two of them had spoken about him, and he couldn't help but wonder what else was said about him while he was sedated. The look on her face was one of surprise, but he expected that, especially since she knew his past so well. He motioned to his injured shoulder.

"Yes, that's how this happened. Sometimes I forget I'm not a teenager anymore, especially when I'm playing basketball with my youth group."

He laughed as he said it, and he blushed from embarrassment as he recalled the idiotic way he tried to show off while playing basketball with the youth and ended up landing hard on his shoulder and tearing his rotator cuff.

"Do you have someone at home to help you while you recover?"

He couldn't tell if she was asking out of curiosity over a relationship or if it was just the nurse in her wanting to know he would be taken care of. He glanced at her left hand and his spirits lifted when he noticed she wasn't wearing a wedding ring.

"No one at my house to speak of, but I live right next door to Bro. Troy and Mrs. Elizabeth, and they've offered to help me. The youth and other members of our congregation have been such a big help too. I have no doubt I'll be well taken care of."

She smiled a bit more broadly when he said no one lived with him...or else the drugs were making him lucid and he was imagining it.

"I've heard of Conway Baptist Church. A couple of my coworkers are members there, and they do a lot of missionary work overseas. They've tried many times to talk me into joining them."

Before he could reply, the curtain opened wide and Mrs. Elizabeth appeared with a male nurse and an empty wheelchair. As badly as he wanted to go home and sleep, he wanted even more to stay put and talk to Roni. There was still so much he wanted to know about her life since they'd parted ways. He'd always dreamed of the day they'd see each other again, but this reunion was far too short for his liking.

"Ready to go, dear?"

He smiled at Mrs. Elizabeth, but he didn't make a move.

"Roni and I were just talking about the medical outreach team from church and their trips."

Just as he expected, her eyes lit up and her attention turned to Roni, which he knew would grant him at least a couple more minutes with her. She reached over and grabbed Roni's hands.

"Oh, sweetie, you should come to our evening service this Sunday. They'll be discussing their upcoming trip to Honduras, and I know they would love to have you there. Please say you'll come."

He knew better than anyone just how persuasive Mrs. Elizabeth could be, and Roni glanced back and forth between them several times before nodding hesitantly.

"I'll see what I can do," she replied.

He hoped she was serious, but he'd heard that type of reply many times before, and he knew it basically meant she wasn't promising anything but just trying to pacify them without hurting their feelings.

"Now, let's get you into this wheelchair so you can go home and get some rest," Roni said. "Did Joanie discuss your after-care instructions with you?"

He and Mrs. Elizabeth both nodded as they helped him get up and move toward the wheelchair. As soon as he stood up, the room started spinning, but thankfully he managed to make it to the wheelchair without falling and humiliating himself. Before the nurse could wheel him away, he grabbed Roni's hand and held on tight.

"I hope this isn't the last time we see each other. I've missed you."

He probably sounded pathetic and desperate, but the last thing he was concerned about was his pride. He wished the circumstances were different and he wasn't injured, so he could have more control over the situation, but right now he was at the mercy of doctors' orders, pain medication, and not to mention Mrs. Elizabeth.

Roni didn't reply, but she gave him a wistful smile that made his heart ache, because it felt like she was saying goodbye...again. He let go of her hand as the nurse turned him around in his wheelchair and proceeded toward the exit.

Mr. Troy and Mrs. Elizabeth talked nonstop throughout the long drive home, but he was lost in his own thoughts and didn't hear most of the conversation. He refused to believe God would answer his prayers and bring Roni back into his life only to rip them apart again.

No, this couldn't be the end.

* * * *

Veronica twirled her pasta around her fork and pushed it absentmindedly back and forth on her plate. For five days, she hadn't been able to focus on anything except her visit with Wyatt. There was something different about him that she couldn't quite put her finger on, and it wasn't just the physical changes either. He seemed...at peace, maybe? She shook her head. No, that didn't make sense.

Veronica stabbed at her spaghetti and sighed as she tried aimlessly to sort through the many different emotions that had plagued her since he left the clinic. Why did seeing him bother her so much? It wasn't like they had ended their relationship on friendly terms, and she had plenty of reasons to never want to speak to him again.

"Veronica?"

Startled from her reverie, Veronica dropped her fork on her plate and sat up straight in her seat. Phil sat across from her, holding two glasses of wine. She looked around at the other couples in the crowded restaurant, and she wanted to kick herself for letting her thoughts about Wyatt interrupt what was supposed to be a romantic dinner.

She took the glass he offered, but she set it on the table instead of taking a sip of wine.

"I'm sorry. I guess I was distracted." she asked.

Phil set his glass down and leaned forward on his elbows to peer at her more closely.

"You've been unusually quiet tonight. Is something wrong?"

Veronica reached across the table and held his hands. He looked so handsome in his suit and tie. It was rare for them to both be off work at the same time and she felt guilty for letting something trivial like seeing Wyatt McDevitt ruin the night.

"I'm fine. It's just been a hectic week at work. What were you saying?"

Phil immediately dropped her hands and sat back in his seat. It was as if a light switch had been turned on because he went from concern for her well-being to talking about himself in roughly two seconds flat. Veronica put her hands on her lap and tried to act enthusiastic as he gushed over his most recent award.

"I wanted to tell Director Montgomery he was lucky I didn't throw the award back in his face, especially since they overlooked me two years in a row. I still can't believe they gave it to Sidney Carson last year. I mean, come on...what has he done? He hasn't performed nearly the amount of surgeries I have since I moved here."

Veronica shifted uncomfortably in her seat. There were moments when his high opinion of himself left a bitter taste in her mouth, and this was quickly turning into one of those moments. She took a deep breath to try and maintain her composure and not yell at him.

"I believe that particular award is given based on merit and not the number of surgeries on a resume," she noted. "Dr. Carson did a lot of volunteer work when he was part of Doctors Without Borders."

Phil shook his head and held up a hand to stop her from saying anything further.

"That's ridiculous," he remarked. "Like those things actually matter."

Veronica bit her tongue. She was honestly stunned. How was it possible she had spent so much time with this man and never noticed how conceited and arrogant he was? Had she been completely blinded by his good looks? Perhaps it was his stature that attracted her so much. She couldn't help but wonder if people thought of her differently because she was with him, especially if they knew his personality.

"How can you say that, Phil? Do you have boundaries when it comes down to whose life you'll save?"

His jaw slacked open as if he couldn't believe she was disagreeing with him. A couple sitting close to them turned to stare, but she was beyond caring at that point.

"Why are you so upset?" he replied. "I thought you were happy for me. I could get a better reception from the women at work."

Veronica's temper bristled as she stood up and threw her napkin on top of her plate.

"Then perhaps you should date them."

Without another word, Veronica grabbed her purse and left the restaurant so she could hail a taxi. She had wondered for five days what it was about Wyatt that left such a lasting impression on her and within just a matter of minutes spent dealing with Phil it was now abundantly clear.

* * * *

Wyatt sat in the front pew of Conway Baptist Church and listened intently as several doctors and nurses from their congregation discussed their upcoming mission trip overseas. Some of the kids from his youth group were also going, and it made his heart swell seeing how excited they were.

For the millionth time that evening, he turned sideways in his seat and looked around the packed auditorium, hoping to find Roni sitting in the audience, but she was nowhere to be seen. He frowned. The room was packed to overflowing, so if she *was* there, he probably wouldn't be able to find her anyway.

Since leaving the clinic and having to spend his days lying in bed recuperating from his surgery, he'd had far too much idle time on his hands. Every waking thought was centered on Roni, and his hopes faded with each passing day he didn't hear from her.

He knew he was probably acting like some love-struck teenager, but he couldn't help himself. If he was physically able, he knew without a shadow of a doubt he would've been back at the clinic searching for her the day after his surgery. He sighed as he looked down at his arm in the sling. Knowing he had at least six weeks of physical therapy ahead of him didn't brighten his mood either.

When the crowd broke into a raucous round of applause, Wyatt cleared his thoughts and refocused his attention on what was happening around him. Bro. Troy called upon him to close the service in prayer, and he got up slowly and made his way to the stage. The terrible pain he'd felt for two days following the operation had finally dwindled to a dull ache, but there were still moments when he had to stop and take a couple of deep breaths to keep the pain at bay. He was used to going full-speed all day long, so having to move at a snail's pace was annoying, to say the least.

Bro. Troy handed him the microphone, and a hush fell over the crowd as everyone bowed their heads while Wyatt led them in prayer. The mood in the auditorium was palpable. People were excited about doing the Lord's work and the feeling was contagious. When he said "amen", the crowd broke into another thunderous round of applause, and as he thanked everyone for coming, he saw a familiar face near the back row.

Veronica.

His heart skipped a beat as he watched her get up and follow the crowd out the front door. He knew there was no way he would be able to reach her if he tried to fight his way through the auditorium, so he sneaked out one of the side doors. He moved as fast as his feet would allow him too, which didn't feel very fast. When he rounded the corner of the church, he saw Roni standing on the sidewalk, attempting to hail a cab.

"Roni!" he yelled. "Wait!"

When she looked in his direction, he motioned for her to stop, and he reached her side as quickly as he could to keep her from bolting. He noticed right away her makeup was smeared and her eyes were bloodshot, as if she'd been crying, which alarmed him immediately.

At first, he didn't know what to say or do, and when she put her arms around him and hugged him, he was completely taken by surprise. He couldn't hold her as closely as he wanted to because of his injured arm, but she was *IN* his arms, and for the time being that was enough. When he discovered she was trembling, he squeezed her tight.

"Roni, what's wrong?" he whispered.

She pulled back and glanced around them at the people who were continuing to file out of the church. There were fresh tears on her cheeks and before she had the chance to object, he gently wiped them away.

"Is there somewhere we can talk privately?" she asked.

He placed a hand against the small of her back and turned her away from the busy street.

"Follow me."

The only place within walking distance was the church, but he knew it would be too crowded inside, so he led her to the playground behind it, which had recently been constructed for the kids at the church daycare center Mrs. Elizabeth managed during the week. Wyatt walked toward a picnic table situated near the entrance. He expected Roni to side on the opposite side from him, but she sat down beside him instead, which made his heart beat a little faster.

She was dressed up in high heels and a navy-blue dress that brought out the blue in her eyes. Her hair hung loosely around her shoulders and she had on several pieces of what appeared to be very expensive jewelry. She looked as if she'd just been to the opera instead of church. He glanced down at his loafers, jeans, and long-sleeved dress shirt and suddenly felt oddly out of place.

"You look beautiful," he remarked.

She smiled at him, but it was a weary smile and not her usual one that could light up any room she entered.

"Thank you," she replied. "I had dinner earlier with my boyfriend, Phil, at Clover's Restaurant."

His heart sank. He wondered if she might be dating someone and now he knew. Apparently, this Phil person was also well off, since Clover's was one of the most expensive restaurants in downtown

Atlanta. He didn't know how to respond, or if he even trusted himself to speak without getting emotional and looking like a fool.

"I guess I should say ex-boyfriend. I saw a side of him tonight that I've tried for two years to make myself believe wasn't there, but...it's over."

Wyatt felt conflicted. He wanted to be excited over the fact that she wasn't seeing him anymore, but it was obvious her heart was broken, and that made his own heart ache.

"I'm so sorry. I can tell you're upset..."

She sat up straight and furiously shook her head.

"Oh, no. That's not the reason for these tears," she adamantly replied. "This is because of something else entirely different."

Okay, now he was really confused. He didn't know what to say, so he just remained quiet and hoped she would elaborate on whatever it was that was troubling her so much. She tilted her head back and glanced up at the stars.

"For almost a week now, I've been trying to figure out what's different about you," she began. "When I talked to you at the clinic I could tell something had changed in your life since we were together. I wasn't going to come tonight, but I'm glad I did, because I found my answer."

He furrowed a brow. "What do you mean?"

She looked at him and smiled.

"While I was listening to those doctors and nurses talking about the mission trips they've been a part of, I felt excited for them. They're joy is hard to miss, and it's not just because they're able to help people in need. You can tell they genuinely love what they do, and that's what I saw in you – happiness and contentment. Being a part of this church family and ministering the youth has changed you, but in a very good way."

He tilted his head and gave her a curious look.

"But why has that made you sad?"

She scooted closer to him and reached for his hand. When she laced her fingers through his, the warmth of her touch made his heart thump erratically.

"It doesn't make me sad, Wyatt. To be honest, I thought I might never see you again after we broke up because you stayed in so much trouble and you seemed so lost. To see you now and the way you've turned your life around...I couldn't be happier for you. I mean that."

He squeezed her hand and tenderly traced her skin with his thumb.

"Then why are you crying?"

She didn't answer him right away, and he didn't push. He would've waited forever if it meant they could stay there together underneath the stars. It felt so good being close to her again. He was right where he belonged.

"I'm crying because listening to your friends tonight and hearing you pray made me realize just how much I'm missing out on. I love my job at my dad's clinic, but for the longest time now I've felt like it's not enough. I want the same contentment and happiness that you have."

Wyatt smiled.

"I want you to have that too," he said. "All I've ever wanted is for you to be happy."

She looked up at the stars again. He felt the strongest urge to pull her close and kiss her, but he resisted it. After all, she'd just broken up with her boyfriend. Although he wanted it more than the air he breathed, he was determined to give her space if it meant there might be a chance for them to be together in the future.

"A couple of days ago, I mentioned to my dad about seeing you at the clinic."

Wyatt shuffled his feet on the ground, remembering how much the man disliked him while he and Roni were dating. At the time, he couldn't understand why, and it made him angry, but it began to make sense as he got older. Mr. Lansing had Roni's best interests at heart, like any normal father would.

"Uh oh," he replied with a smile. "I bet that went over like a lead balloon, didn't it?"

Roni laughed.

"It wasn't that bad. He got a little defensive at first, but when I explained to him what you were doing now he calmed down. He's mellowed out a lot in his old age."

That made him laugh, perhaps a little bit too hard, as he felt a twinge of pain course through his injured shoulder, which didn't go unnoticed by Roni. Jumping up from the seat, her nursing instincts kicked in as she started fussing over his sling, making sure it was adjusted accordingly and not pinching him in any way.

"I'm so sorry. I should've asked you how you were feeling. You really should be resting instead of sitting here with me."

He wanted to stop her, but she looked so adorable when she was worrying over him. Wyatt put a hand under her chin and tilted her head back so he could gaze into her beautiful blue eyes.

"I firmly believe God had His hand in bringing us together again, and I promise you there's nowhere I'd rather be right now than here with you."

When she leaned over to kiss him, he held his breath in anticipation. He wasn't expecting it, but it was a wonderful surprise. Her lips were so soft, and it was as if no time had passed between them at all. It felt every bit as right kissing her in that moment as it did the first time they kissed in 11th grade.

"Is it too soon for me to say I hope you'll be there with me as I make these new changes in my life?" she whispered.

Wyatt stood up and pulled her close so he could kiss her again.

"I'll be with you every step of the way" he promised.

* * * *

Veronica handed her suitcase to the bus driver as he loaded the undercarriage with everyone's belongings. The huge charter bus was one of three transporting members from Conway Baptist and other churches in the community to the airport. People were scrambling in every direction, and the excitement in the air was intense.

"Are you sure you want to do this?"

Veronica gave her dad a big hug and told him "yes" for the hundredth time that morning.

"Dad, we're just going to Honduras for two weeks. I'll be home before you know it, so stop worrying."

She noticed Wyatt standing several feet away, and she waved her hand in the air to get his attention. When he got closer, she noticed he was carrying three Styrofoam coffee cups in a carboard carrier. Her heart melted, which wasn't unusual. He'd done numerous things to warm her heart during their three months together, and it made her realize time and time again just how lucky she was.

Her dad glanced at the charter bus with a nervous expression on his face.

"Promise me you'll look out for her," he said to Wyatt.

She smiled as Wyatt grabbed his hand and gave it a reassuring shake. "I promise."

In the beginning, both of her parents had been understandably leery of their rekindled relationship, but with time they began to see the positive influence they had on each other until they couldn't imagine her being with anyone else.

"In case I haven't said it already, I'm very proud of you both and what you're doing."

His sweet sentiment made her tear up and they both hugged him one last time before the mission director announced it was time to board the buses for the airport.

"I love you, dad," she whispered in his ear.

He kissed her cheek and they wrestled their way through the crowd to their designated bus. Veronica grabbed a seat by the window and

Wyatt sat down beside her. Several minutes later the driver slowly pulled away from the curb, and she waved to her dad one last time.

Wyatt grabbed her hand and squeezed it as they settled into their seats and got comfortable.

"Are you excited?" he asked.

Veronica leaned over and gave him a quick kiss. Yes, she was excited – for their mission trip to Honduras, for their future together...for so many reasons.

"More than you'll ever know."

TO LOVE AGAIN

NIKKI FISHER

Chapter 1

Tick-tock, tick-tock – the wall clock sounded, announcing each painstaking minute that passed by since the day Alec lost his beloved wife, Elvira. It was like all the other priceless items in the house she loved so dearly, which all still stood exactly as it was when she was alive. Alec even went as far as polishing the brass and copper ornaments daily, just like his wife always did, although he hated the smell of the polish.

Tonight was their anniversary and Alec found himself sitting outside on the porch staring out into the distance with Elvira's cat, Storm on his lap. On the side pedestal stood a framed photo of his wife and next to it an unopened bottle of Tennessee Whiskey. Elvira hated the bottle and always threatened to throw it away, but that bottle had some significance to Alec. It was more than just whiskey; it was an unspoken promise to both him and her, to never touch another drop of alcohol again. If it wasn't for Elvira's love and perseverance to help him give up the worst habit a husband can have, he would never have gotten clean. He was an alcoholic for several years, even before he married his one and only true love. At first it was just the odd glass or two a night, then it became one or two bottles a week and before he knew it he was hiding half jacks in the garage, the laundry and even under the seat in his truck. When she first accused him of being an alcoholic all hell broke loose, but eventually reality dawned on him especially the day she stood on the porch waiting for him, her bags were packed and she was ready to leave. At that point their house was up for foreclosure since they could no longer afford the bond payments. It had gotten so bad that they had sold all but the clothes on their back and he was on the verge of losing his job. That was the day he decided to either change or lose it all.

He ran his hand along Storm's soft coat and she purred loudly stretching her front paws elegantly over his lap.

"You miss her don't you?" he said and scratched Storm under the chin.

"I miss her too," he said and carefully lifted Storm off his lap and placed her on the chair next to him.

Elvira found her in a storm water drain one night during a thunder storm, and out of the entire litter of kittens she was the only survivor. The two were inseparable from that day, and now Storm was the only living link he had to his wife. Her soft purring always provided comfort when he needed it the most. At night she always slept at his feet, or on top of him keeping him company.

"Time for dinner Storm, come along," he said and got up. He placed the bottle of whiskey on back on the shelf where it always stood and headed to the kitchen.

He had prepared Elvira's favourite meal, roast chicken and butternut with some brown rice, and tonight he was going to share it with Storm. I shredded some of the white meat off the chicken and placed it in a side plate then lifted Storm unto the table. Storm rubbed against his leg, doubled back and rubbed against him again while she meowed. Alec bent down and scooped her up in his arms and placed her on the table.

"There you go Storm, we're celebrating tonight."

Storm picked at the chicken scraps and purred contentedly while Alec stared at his food and then at the empty chair in front of him. He missed her more than anything.

"I wish you were here my love," he whispered into the silence. He no longer felt like eating and shoved his plate aside.

He simply could not comprehend how life could be so cruel, why would God give you someone to share your life with and then take them away so early?

He met his wife when he was twenty four at a New Year's party. The moment he laid eyes on her he knew she was the one. She was only twenty and a year later on her twenty first birthday he asked her for her hand in marriage. Little did he know that ten years later he would have to let her go of her in the worst way possible. She was only thirty five years old then and had so much she still wanted to accomplish.

He reached out and pulled the newspaper clipping closer, it was the clipping that made headline news after a drunk driver slammed into a car killing two passengers and injuring the driver severely. It was so ironic since he too was once in the same place, an alcoholic with little regard for road rules. Elvira was the driver; she was airlifted to hospital with severe head and back injuries. Three days later he had to make the call to turn off her life support after she was declared brain dead. He remembered it like yesterday, when he sat next to her bed. Although cuts and bruises marred her beautiful face, she had a peaceful expression. He prayed every night for a miracle but that miracle never came and when the doctor told him that there was nothing more they could do, his entire world was sucked into a black hole.

Alec closed his eyes and rubbed his hands down over his face, wiping away the tears. It's been a year since that day, and still he had no idea how he was going to be able to pick up the pieces and move on past that horrific day.

Chapter 2

Laura looked at the bills lying in front of her and shook her head, how was she ever going to make ends meet at this rate? The payments she were able to make to cover her debt was hardly enough to cover the interest and no matter how often she paid she just couldn't get ahead. She should have insisted on alimony from Jeff instead of letting him get away with everything. But at the time of the divorce all she wanted was to close that chapter of her life and never think of him again. She wanted nothing from him, not even a penny. It's been six months since the divorce was finalized but almost a year since she walked into her home to find that other floozy who was old enough to be her daughter in his arms. She never suspected a thing, in fact everything was normal and Jeff even took her out to dinner two nights prior to that to celebrate their anniversary. Mental images of her discovery plagued her for weeks after that and although they became less as time passed by, they did pop up every now and again reminding her how naïve she was all that time she poured her heart into that doomed marriage.

She shoved the envelopes and bills back into the drawer and reached for her keys, at least she had a job, it could have been worse. It was nothing extravagant, and it took her some time to learn how to manage her money and turn over every hard earned cent to make ends meet. But at least this put food on the table and it was a rewarding job. Before her divorce she used to help out at The Ark a pet shelter for lost and abandoned animals whenever she had a spare moment, but after the divorce this place with its animals and caring staff is what helped her pull through. When David Winchester, the owner of the shelter and his wife offered her a permanent position, she didn't think twice. She jumped right in and took charge of her life.

"Good morning Elle, any news on the German Shepherd we found last night?" Laura said as she walked into the reception area.

"Afraid not, he is still at the veterinary clinic for observation. They are considering amputation but it's too early to tell," Elle said as she worked her way down the list of reported strays, "Oh and Snowball had her litter, but unfortunately she didn't make it. Joseph has been feeding them every two hours since last night," she looked up at the clock and then back at Laura, "They are due for their next feed in fifteen minutes, you think you can handle that?"

"Sure I can," Laura said and clocked in her time before making her way through to the cattery, where she found Joseph with the kittens.

"Hello Miss Laura," Joseph said as he carefully laid the little hairless kitten with the rest of the litter, "Miss Elle said you are going to take care of them today."

"Hey Joseph, yeah I am. Poor Snowball, it's so sad that she didn't make it," she said and sat down on the floor next to Joseph crossing her legs, "What happened?"

"The vet reckons she was anaemic and bled out to quick when she was in labour, she would never have made it," Joseph said as got to leave.

"Poor thing, well you have a good day Joseph, I'll see you later then."

"Good day Miss Laura," he said tipping his hat.

Laura looked down at the pink hairless kittens, all with their eyes closed and crawling blindly over each other. They were completely oblivious to the dangers that lurked around them. As she sat looking at them she once again thought how lucky she was that she and Jeff never had any kids. She had seen the adverse effects divorces had on children. Innocent victims having to deal with such adversities like custody battles and which parent to stay with. Maybe if she was able to have kids things would have been different, she thought as she picked up one of the kitten, holding the rubber teat against its mouth. Jeff always wanted kids but she couldn't have any and after various failed attempts he eventually gave up trying too. And although he was adamant that it wasn't important, she couldn't help but wonder at times if it wasn't that, that finally broke the bow.

She blamed herself for everything that went wrong, and she still did, although Elle always reminded her that love is unconditional and if Jeff really did love her, he would have loved her with her faults and failures. Elle and David was a pillar of strength in her darkest days, always motivating her and reassuring her that none of it was her fault.

Chapter 3

It's been raining for two days non-stop, Alec had spent most of the time inside building his custom cuckoo clocks to try and catch up on orders. It was the one thing that kept his mind busy and prevented him from falling into a deep depression. Elvira loved them and always bragged about his carpenter skills. This was just another little thing that kept her memory alive.

He glanced out the window, the world grey and lifeless outside as the mist rolled over the small pond outside the house, the weather was as miserable as he was. He finished touching up the paint on the one clock and placed the brushes in the water before wiping his hands clean. He glanced over at a photo of his wife and Storm and it suddenly dawned on him that he hadn't seen the cat since the day before, but then again he probably didn't pay much attention either.

"Storm, here kitty, kitty!" he called as he walked through the house, expecting Storm to come sauntering out of one of the rooms as he made his way to the kitchen, "where are you hiding?" he called again, still nothing.

As he got the kitchen he went straight to the cat food to fill up Storm's bowl but to his surprise Storms food from the day before was still untouched. Now he was really starting to get worried. He walked through the house looking in every room and under the beds, even in the linen closet where Storm often used to sleep but she was nowhere. The only other place to look was the garage. He pulled on his parka and a pair of gumboots and headed outside. The heavy rain had stopped and all that remained was a slight irritating drizzle that spluttered fine rain drops in his face.

"Storm!" he called over and over but there was no sign of Elvira's cat and here was also no sign of her in the garage. A sense of dread filled him as he started to walk around the house. What if she was caught in the storm last night, or what if a wild animal found her? It wasn't like Storm to wander either.

After almost an hour, Alec headed back into the house. He would start by phoning the local veterinary clinics to see if anyone may have brought Storm in, hoping he would find her. The thought of losing Storm was as bad as the thought of forgetting Elvira. A few calls later he was almost beside himself, no-one has seen Storm. Some suggested that she will find her way back home, but what if she was injured or worse, what if she was dead.

The last vet he called suggested that he contacts The Ark and see if Storm was at the cattery, and although it was at the other side of town, he had to try. He couldn't bear the thought of losing Elvira's cat.

Chapter 4

Laura spent most morning with the kittens and in between feeding times she would pay attention to the other cats, sometimes even end up talking to them as if they would understand her. The best part of it was that they could never gossip, unlike the women she once considered to be her friends. When all the wheels came off, they were the first to run off and tell tall tales about how she failed. Of course Jeff with his charming ways had them all eating out of the palm of his hand anyway, so it was only natural that they would have found the fault with her.

"You've been quiet," David said appearing beside her with a wheelbarrow full of hay.

"Oh no, I'm just tending to the kittens. They feed every hour or two," she said and smiled.

He set the wheelbarrow down and looked at her, "You know, life goes on eventually, but the more you sit contemplating all ifs and ifs-not the longer it takes to heal."

"I'm not blaming myself," she said and laughed half-heartedly.

"Okay, well Elle wanted to know if you'd like to come for dinner, she's worried about you."

"Sure, that will be nice," she responded while tucking the one kitten in with the rest and lifting the other one, "I'll be there at around six?"

"See you then," David said and then went ahead to the chicken coops.

Although she truly appreciated the support she got from David and Elle, she sometimes just needed her space, but either way, being on her own was probably not the best idea. Her thoughts were interrupted when she heard voices approaching; she set the last kitten down with the litter and stood up.

"Miss Laura, this is Mr Bernhard, he's looking for his cat that went missing about two days ago, I don't recall any new strays being brought in, but I told him he's welcome to take a look," one of the staff said.

She smiled and extended her hand, "Welcome to The Ark Mr Bernhard."

"Thank you," he said and looked around, "Those are new born kittens," he commented and went down on his haunches next to them.

"Yes, their mother didn't make it so we're just bottle feeding them until they are ready to be rehomed. So you've lost your cat?" she asked curiously and took the clip board with the list of cats that were brought in, in the past week.

"Yes, she hasn't been home for two days now, and I'm a bit worried. I called all the veterinary clinics in the area but no one has seen Storm," he said stroking the little kittens one at a time.

"Storm is a nice name, what does she look like?" Laura asked.

"She's a ginger tabby, my wife named her after she found her in a storm water drain when she was only a few weeks old," he said and she could hear the sadness in his voice.

"That's a fitting name. When was the last time you saw her?" she asked and paged through the list.

There was a brief silence and she asked again, "Mr Bernhard? When was the last time you saw her?"

"Two nights ago, I was celebrating our anniversary. Elvira would have been devastated if anything happened to Storm," he said quietly.

"I'm sure we'll find her before your wife realizes she's gone," she said reassuringly.

"My wife is no longer around," he said and stood up.

When he turned to look at her she could see the sadness in his steal grey eyes and her heart ached for him.

"I'm sorry, I was out of line," she apologized quickly and hooked the clipboard back on the wall.

"It's quite all right," he started, "she passed away a year ago and Storm was hers. It's the only living thing I have that reminds me of her."

Laura was touched by his openness to share such a sad event with her, a complete stranger, and for some reason she felt indebted to help him find Storm. She may not have experienced the same loss he had, but she knew exactly what loss can do to a person. In some ways they're pain was very similar. On impulse she reached out and touched his arm, "Storm will come back. Cats have a tendency to wander off but they always find their way back to their owners."

He smiled at her and unexpectedly laid his hand over hers, "I hope so," he said and quickly removed his hand.

"Leave your number with me, and if anyone brings in cat that matches Storms' description I will give you a call," she reassured him, "You can also leave a copy of your driver's license at reception to keep on record."

She took down his details and by the time he left, she had already made up her mind to do her best to find Storm. For some strange reason she felt it her duty to help him, even if all that accomplishes was to erase the sadness in his eyes.

Chapter 5

Alec spent the next three days driving around the area trying to find Storm, and with each passing moment, hope also faded. It wasn't like Storm to stray so far off from home that she couldn't find her way back. He was tempted to call The Ark and find out if they have heard anything but for some reason it felt awkward. Although he was desperate to find Storm, he wasn't so sure if his call to The Ark was solely for that. When he met Laura in the cattery, there was a strange stirring deep down that felt like betrayal and he couldn't quite pin down why. She was a beautiful woman, with long brown hair and dark brown eyes that were slightly sunken in. She couldn't have been much younger than him, yet she looked as if she's had her fair share of pain and heartache.

Finally he gave up and picked up the phone to call The Ark, but to his disappointment Laura was not available and the receptionist wasn't able to give him any information either. So instead of waiting around he decided to go there in person. All the way there he convinced himself that he was only interested to find Storm, it had nothing to do with the brown eyed women whose eyes seemed to have mirrored his loss, but the closer he got the more nervous he became.

By the time he reached the pet shelter he was ready to go back home, but a force beyond his understanding moved him into action and he got out of his truck instead. The receptionist was friendly and very helpful reassuring him that Storm will soon turn up, but instead of sending him on his way, she offered to take him through to the cattery to take a look around anyway. Just like the day he firsts got here, Laura was sitting cross legged with her back against the wall, gently feeding one of the small kittens.

"Mr Bernhard, what a pleasant surprise," she said. Her eyes lit up and he quickly dismissed it as his imagination playing tricks on him.

"You can call me Alec," he said half smiling as he stood with his hands in his pockets, "I was just wondering if anyone's brought Storm here yet?"

She didn't move from her spot, simply placed the one kitten down and picked up the next, "No unfortunately not, but as soon as I'm done here I'm going out to visit a few regular places where we normally pick up strays, would you like to ride along?"

Alec was hesitant, going with her felt like he was betraying Elvira, but then again, it was a harmless drive around to find Storm, "Sure, if it won't be too much trouble," he said instead and then also sat down opposite Laura.

"I won't be long, I have three more to feed and we'll be on our way," she said and smiled softly at him.

Alec spotted another small bottle with a rubber teat and without asking he reached for it and picked up one of the kittens holding the teat against its mouth, "My wife used to feed Storm the same way when we found her. She loved mothering the little feline," he started and told Laura how they came to find Storm. It was the first time since the accident that he felt comfortable talking to someone and stranger than fiction he didn't feel morbidly sad. It was as if all these thoughts he locked away suddenly flooded to the sluices of his mind to find an escape route.

The more the spoke of Elvira and Storm the lesser the pain became. It was the strangest thing, and before he knew it, the kittens were fed and they were making their way to the shelter's van.

"You sure it's not too much trouble to ride along?" he asked again as they reached the vehicle.

"I'm sure, besides, it will be nice to have some company," she said and hopped in behind the steering wheel, "buckle up."

Alec chuckled and buckled up and as they drove out of the property he silently apologized to Elvira for feeling happy.

Chapter 6

Laura felt strange about the whole thing, for the first time since Jeff cheated on her she didn't feel any animosity to the general male population. Here next to her sat a man who had his fair share of sorrow and she simply couldn't see him as a cruel manipulative male individual who cared only for his own gain.

"So how did you end up working at The Ark?" he asked her and she smiled.

"It's a long story but since we have time..." she started and turned on the radio.

"Background music for special effects?" he asked laughing.

"Of course we need background music. Well you see, before I was down in the dumps, I was up with the trumps, doing my duty volunteering and... oh bother," she laughed, "I clearly can't do spoken word poetry, so long story short, I used to volunteer when I was married, and after the divorce I just became a permanent feature. It all worked out in the end."

Alec watched her as she drove staring dead ahead and although she was all smiles he noticed sadness in her eyes. It was an emotion that was all too familiar. Loss, a parasite that slowly drained a persons' life force until there was nothing else left to drain.

"I'm sorry for your loss," he said quietly and then looked out the window at the scenery passing by.

"He left me for a woman old enough to be our daughter," she said out of the blue and Alec knew she needed to get it off her chest. Sometimes sharing your sorrows with a complete stranger brought more reprieve than sharing it with someone you knew, and he understood that better than anyone. She told him everything, from the time she caught them in the act to the time she finally walked away and started to pick up the pieces of her life.

"The animals help me realize the importance of life," she finally said as she pulled into a fuel station.

"They do, Elvira always insisted that our souls are linked to our pets in some way, I guess that's why I am so desperate to find Storm."

He felt Laura's hand on his arm and he looked at her.

"We'll find Storm, I have a good feeling about her," she said and then got out of the van, "I just need to get fuel, would you mind handling that while I grab us some coffee?"

Before she could make her way across to the store she ducked in behind the truck and clutched her heart.

"What's wrong?" Alec asked worriedly.

"It's Jeff, oh my dear, I-I can't face him, not now," she said and took a few deep breaths.

"Your ex?" he asked.

"Yes and his girlfriend."

Laura couldn't believe her bad luck, of all places they could go, they had to be here. She had no idea what to do or how to act around them. The next thing she knew, Alec pulled her out from behind the car draping his arm around her shoulders.

"Come on beautiful, if I don't get that coffee now, I might shrivel up and die," he said, just like that in front of Jeff and Miss Priss. She wanted the earth to swallow her whole but that was a tad too late. Alec dipped his head down and kissed her temple and walked straight past the other couple hardly paying attention to them, but Laura was acutely aware of them.

"Laura?" Jeff said in a surprised tone.

"Just play along," Alec whispered in her ear and spun around, with his arm around Laura's waist.

"H-hi, fancy seeing you here," she managed to say.

"Yeah, fancy that. You know Charlize?" Jeff said and gestured to the young girl clinging to his side.

"Don't I, I mean yes, I remember her," she said in a strained tone.

Alec stepped forward and extended his hand, "G'day mate, I'm Alec, Laura's fiancé."

Kill me now, Laura thought and cleared her throat. All she could do was smile and shrug.

"Fiancé, well I'll be damned, you really moved on quick enough," Jeff said with a hint of sarcasm to his tone.

The audacity, she moved on the fast? She thought ready to leap at him and gouge his eyes out, but instead she wrapped her arms around Alec's neck and kissed his cheek.

"Well love sometimes just happens, and when it does it arrests you without warning," she said sweetly and smiled.

"That's my girl, now if you'll excuse us, we have wedding arrangements to get to," Alec said and pulled her away from the ill-fated couple who were now glaring at each other with bitter discontent.

The moment they entered the store, Alec burst out laughing and Laura stood gaping at him.

"I can't believe you just did that," she said laughing.

"I haven't felt this good in ages; did you see the look on his face?" Alec chuckled.

"Didn't I, he was so shocked," she said still laughing, "Thank you Alec, I don't know what I would have done if I ran into them on my own," she admitted.

"Never be intimidated by people who couldn't spare your heart for a moment," he said and smiled.

The rest of the day, Alec spent with Laura driving through rural areas and abandoned places to try and find Storm. Hope was fading as the weather turned from sunny to over cast, but all the while Laura refused to give up.

Chapter 7

Two weeks have passed, and every day Alec went out with Laura collecting abandoned and abused animals, but still there was no sign of Storm. The more he started helping at The Ark the less he focussed on his own pain and suffering. And although Elvira was not far from his mind, thinking about her no longer caused pain. Instead he felt as if he finally had purpose to achieve something greater. Elvira loved animals, and she always tried to get involved with the pet shelters. *Maybe this was her way of telling him to let go and just be;* he thought as he looked down at the kittens whose eyes started opening.

"You're here early Alec," Laura said as she entered the cattery, "just now management is going to expect you to clock in," she joked and sat down with the kittens.

"Then my plan is working," he joked and picked up the little ginger kitten.

"I really think she's lost for good," Alec said as he cuddled the tiny creature in the palm of his hand.

"You don't know that, I'm going to keep looking for Storm," Laura said and looked up at Alec.

"Or maybe it's just time to let go," he said and put the kitten back.

"I tell you what, we do one last run today, if we don't find her I'll closet he case," she said and he could hear the compassion in her voice.

She really did care, and he was touched by her affection and determination to find storm.

"Okay, one last trip and if we don't find her, then the case is closed," he said.

Much later that morning, they were once again on the road. Laura enjoyed Alec's company and realized that once this case is closed she might not see him again.

"You never talk about your wife," she said quietly and glanced at him.

"She was an amazing woman," he started as he looked out the window, "she was very much like you."

Laura blushed and laughed softly, "I very much doubt that," she said and turned down a small road that lead down to the river.

"She loved animals, she was kind, she always helped where she could," he said and then smiled at her.

"Was she ill?" Laura dared ask and she heard Alec sigh, "Sorry I don't mean to pry," she apologised.

"She wasn't ill; she was in a car accident. A drunk skipped the traffic light and collided with her. They were coming from a fund raiser for homeless children. Two of the occupants in the car died on impact but Elvira was still alive. Three days later I had to make the call to turn off her life support," he said and for the first time he didn't feel morbidly depressed telling her.

"Oh goodness, I'm so sorry, that must have been terrible," she said and placed her hand on his arm, "no one should have to go through such pain."

"I guess it's the way of life," Alec said and smiled at her.

Laura wanted to cry, somehow it felt is if his pain were channelling directly through her. She clutched the steering wheel and fought the tears.

"Are you crying?" Alec asked perplexed.

"No, I mean yes," she said and sniffed, using her sleeve to wipe the tears, "I don't know what on earth is going on with me."

Alec chuckled and took out a handkerchief, "Here you go," he said and offered it to her.

"Men still used these things?" she said and patted her cheeks dry.

"I'm old school."

They drove in silence for a while until they reached a dead end where the river had washed away a part of the road and got out of the van. As usual Alec followed Laura always making sure there were no dangers lurking like rabid animals or criminals for that matter. Nowadays one couldn't be too careful.

"You hear that?" Laura said and stopped in her tracks causing Alec to almost crash into her.

"Hear what?"

"A cat, I hear a cat in distress it's coming from that direction," she said and rushed ahead, treading along the bank of the river.

"Laura, be careful the bank is very slippery," he warned and followed her, hoping that their luck may have turned and that Storm was actually alive.

A few feet along the bank, they finally reached a tree that hung low over the river, and there she was, Storm, clinging to the tree for dear life, completely drenched and shivering. Laura went straight for the Storm, but Alec caught her by her arm.

"Easy there Jane, this tree won't hold you," he warned and pulled her away from the tree. He made it his duty to always carry the first aid kit and rope with him when they ventured away from the vehicle, just in case they ran into any snags, and this was one of them.

"Jane?" Laura said laughing, "Where's Tarzan when I need him?" she joked and raised her arms for him.

"You never know when Tarzan might deem it necessary to make his debut appearance," he said and reached around her to tie the rope to her waist, and for a brief moment he looked into her eyes and stilled. Laura didn't look away from him either, she just stood and waited, but he could have sworn he heard her heart racing in her chest, just like his was racing now.

"If I don't save that cat now, there won't be a later," she whispered.

Alec blinked and shook his head smiling, and fastened the rope around her waist, but before she stepped away from him, he pulled her back, "Please be careful, I don't want to jump into that cold river today, but I will if you end up in it."

Laura smiled at him and then reached up and cupped his cheek, "I'm sure Tarzan will come to Jane's rescue then," she said and stood on her toes to kiss his cheek.

Laura carefully stepped on the bank and made her way along the unsteady branch that jutted out over the river. Each step was carefully calculated. With Alec on the bank pulling on the rope securing her, she felt a little more at ease. The river was starting to rise quickly and she knew she didn't have much time. She looked up-stream to make sure there were no drifting logs or debris coming her way and then she carefully entered the water. The current was strong, tugging roughly at her, just a few more feet and she would be able to reach Storm and save the poor thing.

"Are you still okay?!" she heard Alec call over the rushing waters and she signalled a thumbs-up, but as she did, she lost her footing and slipped. The surge of water instantly dragged her under and she fought to come up for air, but the river was merciless and every time she tried to get up it pulled her under.

Within seconds she felt a hand tug her by her collar and then another coming around her waist pulling her up and she gasped for air.

"Storm!" she cried out in a panic, "I have to save her!"

"Forget the cat, I need to get us to safety," Alec roared as he fought against the rushing waters. A loud crack sounded and the branch crashed into the water with Storm still clutching to the tree. It was too late, she realized as Alec finally dragged her to the river bank. Storm was lost.

Laura fell unto her back and started to sob, but Alec gathered her in his arms and pulled her against him.

"It's okay sweetheart, there's nothing that you could have done to save her," he said and pressed his lips against her forehead.

"I wanted to save her," she sniffed and buried her face against his drenched shirt.

"So did I, but I think she saved us," he said in a soothing tone.

Laura looked up and met Alec's gaze and in that moment she realized exactly what he meant. Alec dipped his head down and pressed his lips against hers and kissed her softly, "I told you I'd jump in if I had to," he whispered smiling against her lips.

"So Tarzan does exist," she said and looked up in his eyes.

Alec knew there and then that nothing ends with death, and when you allow love to heal the pain, there is hope for a better tomorrow.

TO TRUST AGAIN

62

NATASHA GROVER

To trust again...

When Annie's long-time boyfriend decides that the Amish way was no longer his way, she is left shattered, but worst of all single. She struggles to overcome rejection and prays for God to help her, but all she gets in return is silence. Barren and a spinster, she had lost all hope of finding love. But through revelation during a Sunday service, she discovers that there is hope, and that is when everything changes.

When Seth and his daughter Mary arrive in town, everything changes. A chance meeting with a beautiful woman who adores his daughter was nothing but the grand design of God.

God works in mysterious ways, and this is exactly what happens when two souls are meant for each other.

Chapter 1

Annie looked down at the small keepsake box Abel gave her last Christmas. She never thought she would feel this way, so deserted and lost. Abel was the only man she ever cared for and now he was gone, out of her life and out of her world, but still so very present in her mind. She couldn't believe it when he came to her just a month ago to tell her he was leaving for good. Everything seemed so perfect, she was happy; she thought he was happy and although he often told her how he would have liked to be able to study science instead of erecting barns and toil in the fields, she never expected him to follow that farfetched dream of his. After all, his father was the Bishop of Lititz and he knew the consequences of his actions, yet here she was staring eternity in its face with no hope to marry one day. *How could God have allowed this to happen*, she thought as tears welled up in her eyes, surely He would not have allowed such a worldly passion to overcome Abel and allow his servant and son to run into a world where evil is so rife.

"Annie, it's time to let it go," Anke said as she came to stand next to her.

"Not now Anke," Annie mumbled, wiping the tears from her cheeks.

"You've been a walking corpse since he left, you hardly eat and all you do is sit here and sulk, sooner or later the pain will go away, but only if you let it go."

"It's easy for you to say, you have everything," she blurted out and stormed into the house to find the solitude of her room.

Anke was her younger sister, what did she know of heartbreak? It wasn't as if she could simply turn off a switch and stop feeling so terrible. She was married, she had everything Annie ever wanted, she had a loving husband a child and her life was perfect. Anke knew better than to envy her sister, but her emotions were all over the place and right now not in the best of places either. If only she could turn back time and try harder to convince Abel to stay. But now that she had time to think things over it became more and more evident why Abel never proposed to marry her. He never intended to stay, and after Bishop King's passing, there was nothing to stop him from pursuing his dream. If he loved her like he so often said, then why did he break her heart? He didn't even ask her to join him, not that she would have, but if he had asked her then she would have been certain that he did in fact see a future with her, but then it would have been her choice to stay. But instead he went on his own, because he wanted to leave everything behind, including her.

She slammed the door to her room shut and pressed her back up against it, this raging sea of anger was suffocating her in ways unimaginable. She was angry with Abel, with Anke and even with her youngest sister Mabel. Convicted by the thought of being angry even with God, she tossed the keepsake box aside and fell to her knees.

"Forgive me Father; I'm a simple person with a broken heart. Please take away this pain and heartache," she prayed as tears streamed down her face, "Please help me to understand why everything is going wrong in my life. Have I not been a loyal servant?"

She waited expectantly for an answer or for the pain to miraculously disappear, but the silence was like a poison that seeped into her blood and paralyzed her. The emptiness she felt was overwhelming and cruel, "Why have Thou forsaken me?" she cried. It felt as if God had turned his back on her, even though she had no idea why. She searched the recesses of her mind, trying to make sense of it all, trying to remember any sins she may not have asked forgiveness for, but nothing came to mind. Rejected by her one true love and by God, she curled up on the floor and wept.

Chapter 2

Two days have passed, since her melt down in front of her sister, and thankfully Anke did not poke at her again, but the emptiness was far from gone. Numb she sat against the wall in Bishop Troyer's house with everyone else occupying the space for the Sunday Service. She felt almost alienated and the looks of sympathy she got from her peers didn't help her mood either, she was an utter disgrace, not to mention humiliating. All the other women her age was settled down with their own families. And at the age of twenty-nine she had nothing but broken dreams strewn in the wake of a failed relationship.

Caught up in her own thoughts she paid little attention to the service, until Bishop Troyer clapped his hands together and exclaimed loud enough for her to pay attention, "Trust in the Lord with all your heart and lean not on your own understanding; in all your ways submit to him, and he will make your paths straight."

That was her moment of realisation, all this time she had been trying to make sense of it all with her own understanding. And she was too emotional to thing rational, she still had a lot of questions as to why God had taken Abel from her when she was so sure they were promised to one day marry, but if she was going to get through all of this she was going to have to put her trust in God.

After the service she felt less burdened, almost as if a weight had been lifted, the longing was still there but it was lighter than before and instead of going home she took a walk down the small path that led to the a nearby brook. A time for reflection was nigh and by the grace of the Father, she could finally be free. She sat down in grass near the stream and closed her eyes, raising her face to the sun and soaking in it warmth. The spinning chaos that had altered her world over the past month or so was suddenly replaced by hope and for that she was grateful for.

"Daed!" a little voice called not far from where Annie was sitting and she quickly opened her eyes and looked up stream, and then she saw the little girl in her blue dress skipping towards her, and not far behind her, her father or so she would assume.

"Hello," the little girl said as she reached her, "why are you sitting here?"

"Mary, where are your manners?" her father reprimanded when he reached her, "I'm so sorry, she gets out of hand quite quickly," he apologised and Annie simply smiled.

"It's quite alright, I was just enjoying the fresh air," she said to the little girl, "My name is Annie," she smiled and extended her hand to the little girl, who suddenly shyly hid behind her father.

"She's embarrassed now," he chuckled and pulled her out from behind his legs, "Say hello to Annie."

"Hello Annie," the little girl, who couldn't have been older than five or six years greeted, with her thumb stuck in her mouth and her toes pointed to each other.

Annie did not recognize them, although their community was sizable and she didn't know a few people by name, she would surely have remembered the faces. And as far as she can recall she hadn't seen the little girl at the local school where she often helps out as a teacher's aid, but then she may not be six yet.

"I'm Seth," he said and tipped his hat, "Mary likes to come here whenever we come to Lititz."

So they were not from around here, she realized raising her hand to cover the bright sunlight streaming down from above, "Where are you from?"

"Rothsville, we came to attend the church service at least once a year in honour of my belated wife."

Annie's heart cramped in her chest, as she realized he was widowed, yet his tone of voice sounded uplifting as if he had made peace with his loss.

"Mamm died of cancer," little Mary piped up.

She had a maturity level Annie hadn't seen in a child for a long time, and realized that it may be because of her loss.

"My condolences to you," she cleared her throat, "It must be a difficult time for you."

"It's been a year and some months now, Meryl was from here originally, and I promised her that I will bring Mary here, she always liked it here by the stream."

"Why do you come here?" Mary asked again and this time Annie pushed herself up to on to her feet.

"Well I like the stream too, especially the flowers that grow on the banks," she smiled and ironed down the front of her dress, "But I'm done now, so you can play here as long as you want."

"Oh no, you don't have to leave," Seth objected.

Annie smiled at him and shook her head, "I have to get going anyway, and I only came here for a little while to clear my head."

"Why don't you stay?" Mary pleaded and tugged on her hand.

Annie's heart warmed to the little girl, she was adorable. With big blue eyes and blonde curly hair that stuck out from under her bonnet. She was sure that Mary was Seth's ray of sunshine.

"Maybe next time, I have to go and prepare food with my sisters."

"Let go of Annie's hand Mary," Seth instructed his daughter and pried her away, "I'm sure we will meet each other again and then you can invite Mary to join you here at the stream."

"What a lovely idea," she smiled, "maybe I will pack a few eats for the next time you come here."

Little Mary nodded excitedly and Seth simply smiled at her, which caused her tummy to tumble. He was a handsome man, and probably not much older than her. Not to mention his lovely little girl.

"I will see you around some time," Annie said and then waved as she headed up the small path.

What a chance meeting, she thought. Here she was down and out and God had just revealed to her that He is still in control, and then she meets this charming little family, who despite their loss, can still smile and radiate such hope and passion that it could ignite a fire. Just to see them together warmed her heart. She looked back again and smiled as little Mary waved back at her.

Chapter 3

Seth looked at Mary where she played on the edge of the stream, floating leaves like little boats downstream. Every now and again she placed a pebble on one of the bigger leaves and when it didn't sink she squealed excitedly. She reminded him so much of Meryl, her summer blonde hair that curled like her mothers' and the dimples that indented on her cheeks when she smiled. It's been over a year since his wife had passed away from cancer, and although he accepted it a long time ago, he's only now starting to feel human again now. He had been on autopilot since her death, having had to focus on Mary and raising her, in a way he was grateful that he had his little girl. Having someone to depend on him during such a difficult time eased the hurt and pain somewhat. That was the way of life, the weak always cares for the weak, it is how God intended it. He just wishes he could have been able to save Meryl, then she could still be here watching Mary grow up.

He lay back in the grass, hitched up on one arm, He dared not question God, he knew that through the storm, God had a plan and he was going to wait on God to reveal that plan no matter how long it takes.

His thoughts shifted to the woman he had met earlier, she wasn't young enough to be unwed, and she wasn't a widow, but yet she is unattached, which he found strange. A woman with such a beautiful smile would have many possible suitors.

"Seth!" a distant voice drew him out of his reverie.

He looked up and noticed William headed his way. William was one of his friends who lived here, and whenever he came to visit, he stayed with him. He raised his hand and waved, still keeping a vigilant eye on Mary.

"Finding you is no easy task," William said as he reached him.

"You know I bring Mary here right after church whenever I'm in town," Seth said and chuckled as Mary jumped up and down to cheer on her fleet of leaves.

"She's grown up since I last saw her."

"Yes she has, but we haven't been here for some time."

"True," William nodded, "I actually came to ask if you would be up to help us out with a barn rising. Our planner, well he upped and left unexpectedly and we need someone with skill to draw up the plans."

A barn raising, it's been years since Seth had taken part in any of those, the last time he did was over three years prior to his wife's passing. He had to admit, the thought of staying here while longer was tempting. Mary will get to come here every day, he would be able to put his skills to the test, and maybe, just maybe he will be able to get to meet Annie again. That thought crept in there without warning and he quickly cleared his throat and mentally shook his head. There was no time in his life for romance; he had a daughter to care for and a business to run. As a carpenter he prided himself in the work he could do, simple yet sophisticated pieces of furniture, sold not only to the Amish community but also to outsiders who valued solid oak furniture. And with the off cuts he made small ornaments and bird houses which he sold at a local stand just outside Rothsville.

"So what happened to the other chap?" he asked curiously.

"He got tired of our ways and headed out into the world."

"That's a pity, but I guess I can hang around a little longer if you don't mind that Mary and I stay on at your place."

"Of course I won't mind, you're always welcome here you know that."

The sudden jolt of excitement made Seth grin from ear to ear. It looks like this year was a year of the Lord's favour; he will finally get to work on something significant again.

He called for Mary and she quickly came skipping towards him, she was going to be so happy to stay here, he just knew it.

"How would you like to stay here for a few weeks?" he said as he knelt down on one knee, while dusting off dry leaves and grass from her dress.

Her infectious smile spread across her face and her eyes lit up, "Really *Daed*?" she said with her child like enthusiasm, "Will I get to see Annie?"

Taken by surprise that she actually mentioned Annie, he cast a quick glance to William, who stood with his arms crossed and an amused expression on his face.

"She was here at the brook when we got here, Annie likes her," he fibbed for an excuse.

"Sure she does," William smirked.

"Can I daed, can I?" she pleaded as she hopped unto his one knee.

"I'm sure we can make a plan," he said, how could anyone say no to such a face.

As the three of them headed back up the small hill towards civilization, Seth couldn't help but think about Annie, the friendly yet mysterious woman with the radiating smile, who seemed to have captured his daughter's attention. She had never taken to any other woman like this before, not even Grace, Meryl's younger sister.

"A penny for your thoughts," William said and grinned at him.

Seth chuckled and hooked his thumbs into his suspenders, he might as well be out with it, "It's been more than a year since Meryl passed away, sooner or later Mary will need a woman to teach her how to conduct herself appropriately. Teach her how to quilt and bake bread and so on."

"And you're thinking of Annie?" Willian asked as he kicked a stone out of the way.

"Not specifically, but meeting her and seeing how much Mary enjoyed her company made me think about it."

Who was he kidding, of course he was thinking of Annie. He met some other women from his own town who were all too willing to step up and fill Meryl's shoes but he never really paid any attention to their advances. But now out of the blue, all he could seem to think of was her.

She was heaven sent, no doubt and if he didn't at least try, he would never know.

"Ay, well, Annie has had her heart broken and she's been a difficult one to get on with ever since, so good luck."

"Did it happen recently?" he asked curiously.

"About a month ago, you know the planner I told you about? Abel was his name. He just came out one day, said his good byes and left. I believe he went to New York to study science."

"And left her behind too..."

Seth felt a great deal of sympathy for her, and his heart ached. He could only imagine how much pain she must have gone through when that happened. It's one thing to send someone off to the beyond, but having someone leave out of free will to explore the world out there was like a slap in the face.

"Yeah, it was rather sad, they looked happy together."

"Clearly he was not happy, otherwise he would not have broken her heart," Seth defended.

He knew that he was going to have to take one step at a time with Annie, and not push her into anything she didn't want. But if there was one thing he would do for her, whether they ended up together or not, was to show her that God has a plan for all his children.

Chapter 4

The quietness of the early morning was peaceful, there were no birds singing their morning songs or a rooster crowing to announce the start of a new day and the sun was still buried behind the horizon. Annie closed her eyes again as the heady pull of her dreams beckoned her back to play, but she had to wake up. There was too much to do on this blessed day. The past month she spent wallowing in self-pity had robbed her of some precious time such as baking bread and taking it to the local store, not to mention her chocolate cookies everyone always used to love so much. And maybe if she was lucky, she may be able to get some of those cookies to Mary before she departed with her father.

Even for an overcast day, nothing could dispel the mood Annie was in, for the first time in weeks, she felt alive again and ready to take on the world.

"You're up early," Eva said as she entered the kitchen, "and you're baking?"

Annie smiled at her youngest sister and nodded, "Yes, it's time I stop fussing over Abel and get on with life."

Eva ran around the table and threw her arms around her neck, "Thank goodness! We were all getting so worried about you. I'm so glad you've come to your senses."

Annie laughed and hugged her sister back, it's only now that she realized just how much she inconvenienced everyone around her and she was relieved that it had all come to an end. Yes, she may still think of Abel from time to time, but it no longer affected her as it did just a day ago before God had spoken to her heart. And if she can embrace the change with a positive attitude, then she will only be blessed richly.

"I'm sorry I had you all so worried, but it's all in the past now," she said as tears sprung to her eyes.

"No need to apologize, you and Abel were together for a very long time."

Eva released her and reached for one of the cookies on the cooling rack, and then picked up her quilt basket, "I have to go, but when I get back I want to hear how on earth this paradigm shift took place."

"Of course," Annie laughed and swatted her sister's hand away, "These are for Mary, and I'll bake another batch for the house later this afternoon."

"Who's Mary? Oh wait, don't tell me, I'm going to be late, but when I get back later you can tell me everything."

And like a whirlwind Eva left the house.

Later than morning after delivering the baked flat breads to the local store Annie's mood had taken a turn for the worst, but not because of Abel. She had hoped to see Mary and Seth but it seemed that she was too later. The realization that they had left to go back to Rothsville left her empty. She should have asked them when they were leaving instead of putting in all the effort to bake cookies for Mary. A soft sigh escaped her lips as she made her way towards Anke's house, at least the cookies will be put to good use there, she thought.

"Mary!" A little voice called out to her and Anke's heart leapt with joy and she spun around.

"There you are," she smiled, "I thought you had gone back home."

"Oh no, daed said that we'll be staying here while he builds a barn," she exclaimed and hugged Annie's leg.

"She beat me to it," Seth said when he reached them.

Annie's heart fluttered in her chest and she smiled up at him, next to him the top of her head only reached his shoulder. She was just as excited as the toddler clinging to her dress having learned that they will be staying on for a while. Normally Abel would be the one drawing up the plans for the barn and making sure everything was in order. It used to be so exciting watching him loose himself I the work.

"Where will you be staying?"

"We'll be staying with William and his wife; he was kind enough to open his door for us."

"That's good yah," and she went down on her knees to get to Mary's level, "I baked you some chocolate cookies," she said holding out the small tin.

Mary beamed and immediately took the tin from Annie and dug in.

"Thank you Annie," Seth said as she stood up, "Mary has really taken to you."

"She's a lovely child."

For a moment, Annie was lost in Seth's gaze and his smile that could make the world around her fade into the background. Mary had his smile with his dimples as well as his sky blue almond shaped eyes, there was no doubt that she was his daughter. The only difference was that he had he had brown hair. His wife must have been a beautiful woman, she thought briefly before little hands drew her attention again.

"Daed said that I can stay here today while he goes to fetch our clothes, only if I stay with you."

She was so caught up in her own thoughts she never heard that part of the conversation, and the toothy grin Mary gave her arrested her.

"Well, if you don't mind leaving her with a complete stranger, then I'm happy to take care of her for you," she smiled.

"You're not a complete stranger and William did say you were good with children."

So she had been a topic of discussion between him and William? Now more than ever, she was intrigued by Seth. But if she had been the topic of discussion hen surely William had divulged the bit of information about Abel.

"Of course!" she said out loud, "You're here to take over what Abel failed to complete," she blurted out unceremoniously.

"Pardon me?"

"Abel, he used to do the plans for the barns,"

"Oh yes, Abel. That's right. William asked me to help out."

A small frown creased on his forehead and Annie almost kicked herself, that wasn't even the conversation topic. The whole thing was about her taking care of Mary.

"I'll watch Mary for you," she railed back on to the topic, "we're going to have a lot of fun."

"Will you make my hair like yours?" Mary asked and Seth laughed.

"Like mine? But what is wrong with your hair, it looks beautiful."

"It's too curly and dead can never brush it."

She looked back at Seth and he shrugged, "It's always tangled, you have no idea how difficult it is to brush her hair."

"Well I have just the solution for your problem," Annie said grinning.

The poor father had no idea how to raise a daughter, and if she could help in any way she was more than happy to.

Chapter 5

Barn raising day…

It was a fine summer's day, and the weather couldn't be more perfect. The entire community had gathered to do the barn rising for the Yoder family, who had lost their barn in a fire two months ago, and while the women were all busy making food and helping with odds and ends, the men got ready for a hard day of teamwork.

Seth stood at the table at the far side of the grounds looking over his plans again. Although raising a barn was a much bigger project that putting together tables and chairs he was confident that I was flawless.

"So word has it that you're keen on Anny," William said as he came to stand beside him.

"Is that so?" Seth chuckled.

"Yah, yah, I've heard the talk in the town. Her sister Anke actually asked me outright if I knew anything."

Seth crossed his arms over his chest and glanced towards the tables where the women were gathered. There among them all sat Annie with Mary in deep conversation. He had only been here for two weeks, and during this time he had grown fond of her. But there was always the question that poked at his conscience. Was he attracted to her simply because she got on so well with Mary, or was he attracted to her because she was, well, Annie.

"She's a pretty woman, and she's very good with children," Seth admitted, trying not to say too much.

"Come on Seth, it's more than that. She's good with children yah, but she will make a fine wife. You should go on and talk to her."

"I'm sure she does, but I don't know if she is over Abel at all."

That was a truth he could not deny. She had hardly spoken about Abel during their meets at the creek, but the way she reacted that morning when she realized that he had taken the work Abel was meant to do, indicated that he still affected her. And how would he compete with that?

"Trust me, according to Anke, her entire mood changed since the day you arrived, she just needed a shove in the right direction."

"Well at least I accomplished something," Seth joked and elbowed William, "We can jabber on about her later, right now we have a barn to finish. Are the men ready to start?"

William shook his head and chuckled, "They are all ready, but if God wills for you two to get together, you know that no power on earth or in heaven can prevent that, right?"

"Then we shall see what God has in store."

William was right about one thing, if God had his hand in this and the only reason he ended up in this community was to meet Annie, then he prayed that God's will would reign over his fleshly emotions that have been running rampant of late. If not, then he will finish this barn here today, and return to Rothsville a sane but proud father.

By the end of the day the structure stood high against the afterglow of the setting sun, and families were slowly making their way home. Seth was pleased by the work that was accomplished in one day and the fact that he was able to lay out the plans to such perfection made him proud to say the least. With only the Yoder's left along with the odd family friends, Seth made his way to where Mary was helping Annie pack away the excess food. For a moment he looked at the two of them and couldn't help but smile. Annie really did like Mary, and if he had to be honest with himself, he liked her too. She was a beautiful woman with a heart of gold and a soft spot for Mary.

Chapter 6

The barn had finally been completed, and Annie knew all too well that soon she would have to say her farewells to Seth and Mary, and that thought alone left a lump in her throat. She really liked them, especially Mary. Annie swallowed at the lump in her throat; she would never be able to have her own children, not since the unfortunately surgery when she was only twenty that left her barren. And having been able to spend these few weeks with Mary really left her wishing for a miracle.

"You should tell him how you feel," Eva said at the breakfast table.

"You mean Seth?" Annie said blushing slightly.

Eva laughed and reached for Annie's hand, "Everyone can see that you two like each other. He's a widow and you're a spinster, you're simply perfect for each other."

"I would never be so forward!" Annie exclaimed laughing, "If he feels the way everyone assume he feels, then he would have to do the ground work."

Eva raised a brow, "And if he doesn't because he is to shy?"

"Then so be it, but I am not going to embarrass myself, what if everyone is wrong about him?"

"Trust me, we're not wrong."

Eva was persistent, for one she was young and full of happily ever after dreams; secondly, she was a self-proclaimed match maker. But even if Eva was right, Annie simply refused to put herself in the firing line. It would be up to God to guide her way, not her own understanding. Her own understanding when it came to Abel didn't help one bit, so she was going to have to simply put her trust in God and hope for the best outcome.

A slight knock on the door drew the sisters' attention and Eva was the first to rush to open the door and a few seconds later, it was Seth and Mary standing in their kitchen.

"Why don't you two join us for breakfast," Eva invited.

"Oh no, we've already had breakfast," Seth said, never taking his eyes of Annie.

Eva's gaze moved from Seth to Annie and back to Seth, when she raised both brows and fought to hide a smile.

"Mary, come with me, I want to show you my room."

Relieved Annie let out breathless sigh and stood up.

"I suppose you would have to go back to your home now that the Barn is up?"

The way Seth stood shifting his weight from one foot to the other, with his head in his hand made her smile, he looked so nervous. If only he could hear the frantic beating of her own heart.

"Yah, I have to go back. I have a business to run which I have neglected while staying here," he said and looked around the kitchen.

"I'm sorry," Annie said and cleared her throat, "I'm confident that God will help you make up time for your generous act of kindness to help the Yoder's."

Without warning, Seth stepped forward and came around the table until he stood in front of her. Of course her heart stopped and the zooming bees in her stomach did not help her one bit.

"Thank you for helping out with Mary," he said with his eyes downcast.

"That was no problem at all; maybe when you come back, I can help again."

She meant it, every word. She would do anything to spend some more time with Mary and teach her how to bake and quilt. The way she felt now, she wished that this would never end. But what she wished for more was for Seth to tell her how he felt.

"I've actually been thinking," he started and Annie held her breath.

"Yes?"

"Well, you get on so well with Mary, and well, we get on well too..." he paused and shuffled closer, "I know I'm not going about this the right way, but I was thinking or rather wondering if you would like to come with us to Rothsville."

Annie's mouth fell open and she stared at him, "You mean move there?

Seth nodded and shrugged, "We've only known each other for a short while, but when Jacob saw Rachel for the first time, he wanted to marry her right away..."

It felt as if Annie's entire world was turned on its axis and spinning in the opposite direction, did Seth just ask her to marry her or was she misunderstanding the meaning behind his words?

"What exactly are you proposing?" she said in a trembling voice.

"Oh for heaven's sake! He's asking if you'll marry him!" Eva shouted from the passageway.

Just then Mary came running out flinging her arms around Annie's legs.

Seth shrugged and smiled, "In short, yes. I mean I will go the Bishop first to ask for his blessing, but I have grown very fond of you and so has Mary, and after the time we spent together, I've come to realize that God had brought us to this place."

Her eyes shot full of tears and Eva lifted Mary up in her arms, twirling around and cheering, while her and Seth simply looked at each other.

A simple yes was all it took and Annie's dreams had come true. She found love in the strangest of circumstances and when she least expected too. On top of that, she would get to teach Mary everything that is good.

~*~

Seth could hardly have believed it was it not for the fact that he pinched himself for the umpteenth time. But there she stood, in her wedding garments. As beautiful as the first day he saw her near the brook and she was finally going to be his. But he knew that it was only by the hand of God that he had finally found a woman who will be good to both him and his daughter. And that was Annie, beautiful sweet spinster, Annie.

FOR A FIREFIGHTER'S HEART

84

MARISA MEYER

Chapter 1

Christine Rossouw assessed the destruction left behind by the blaze that reduced the Mulders' house to nothing but a pile of rubble and ash. It was pure luck that no one had gotten hurt in the blaze. The fire had started in the early hours of the morning when the Mulders' were still fast asleep. Now they all stood on the sidewalk, with nothing but the clothes on their back and their pet cat Malfoy, looking in horror at what was left of their home. Their belongings and their memories had literally gone up in flames. Now that was something she could never fathom, why would a family who lived day to day, turning over every penny have to endure such hardships? Why could this not happen to someone who could afford it?

It's the Lord's way to test our faith; her father's voice reminded her. To her it was more an excuse used by churchgoers to explain away logic, and logic told her a long time ago, that man's path is not destined or designed by God, but that man's path is a series of truth or dares onramps to new beginnings and disastrous endings.

She ducked under the warning tape that stretched across the front lawn, here and there, there were a few firefighters ambling around, just to ensure that the fire had been completely snuffed. Her job was to investigate the cause of the fire and fill our mounds of paperwork for insurance claims. She stepped over what used to be the threshold of the house, into what was left of it. Everything was charred black, logically, if the Mulders had all been asleep, and still managed to get down the stairs and out the front door, the fire could only have started at the back of the house or possibly the basement. Instinctively she traipsed over the rubble making her way through to the back of the house where the Laundry area used to be.

It took her close to an hour to determine the area where the blaze started and another hour to determine if it was accidental or not. In no time she had drawn the conclusion that the fire started as an electrical short in the laundry area. Apparently, Mrs. Mulder often left her tumble dryer on overnight. This, of course, would make claiming insurance a little more troublesome. Yet another flaw in the system, the insurance company is going to find every reason not to pay out the claim, by basing it on negligence, no wonder people were so up in arms with short term insurance places.

When she finally walked into her office by noon, she was finished, it's been one of those days where you barely get time to drink a cup of coffee, much less have lunch. The thought of lunch made her tummy rumble and she turned left down the hall to where the company's cafeteria was. She never ate here, but today was an exception. She had been up since 4 AM after being called out by the Fire Chief, and right now a greasy Burrito even sounded like heaven.

When she got back to her desk, there was a note that read – *Love me tender love me true, why not date me until you're blue.*

"Okay, guys! Who did it?" she asked as she crumpled up the note and dumped it in the trash.

None of them owned up but all of them laughed behind their sleeves. She knew that they all thought she was the odd one out, not being interested in dating and all. Whenever there was a company function that allowed partners, she went alone. If they all went out to drinks, she went alone. Now, it wasn't because she was anti the whole prospect of dating; it was just that she had no interest in getting tied down to one person who eventually ends up changing your character.

She had seen it so often. People lose their individuality, they change, and not for the better either, and years down the line, one or the other regret the fact that they had changed, and that's when trouble spoils paradise. Obviously, her current outlook on life came at a price. Just out of college, she dated Darryl, who was a very responsible young man with high ideals and in her opinion far-fetched dreams, but he was nice. In the beginning, like every other relationship, they both had different interests, but they both tried to get involved, she went with him to Nascar races, and he went with her to theater performances.

Then they started to get comfortable and suddenly she was going to all the car races, and he came up with every excuse under the sun not to go to a theater. But it got worse, slowly but surely he started to get his back up whenever she went to the theater alone and then they ended up fighting more than anything. It was there when she finally pulled the plug on their relationship and promised herself never to date again, against her mother and fathers' wishes of course.

The ringing of her phone, drew her out of her train of thought and she reached for the receiver, "Rossouw speaking," she answered absentmindedly while she shuffled through the stack of paperwork on her desk.

"Oh, hey dad," she said and pinched the received between her shoulder and her ear. "Mmm no, I haven't forgotten... yeah... mmm... well, I'm kind of busy... I know, I said I would be there but something came up... seriously, dad, it's not like the church is going to run away... Okay fine, I'll be there... yeah, I love you too."

She pulled out the incident report from one of the arson cases she had to submit to the lawyer and shoved it into the out basket, then dropped her head on her arms. She loved her parents, but her dad was forever begging her to go to church. Another place she tries to avoid at all cost. Church people were probably the most hypocritical beings alive, she thought despondently, but she knew that if she went to this one service, they would leave her alone for several months before they begged her to visit again. So she was going to simply suck it up, go, and get it over and done with.

Chapter 2

Jarod looked at himself in the mirror as he fixed his tie, it was still a while before the church would start, but he preferred to be the first one in and the first one out, usually picking the last pew right in the corner. He had a very trying time after his divorce, nearly lost his job and everything he had, because of it. Was it not for Pastor Rossouw who helped him to see the light, he would still be staring at the bottom of the bottle. He was never much of a drinker during his marriage, but after he found out that Elaine cheated on him, he drowned his sorrows, the only way he knew how. It's been two years since they went their separate ways and it was just like Pastor Rossouw had said, his hatred had turned to indifference, and the love he once felt for Elaine had subsided. He often saw her in town, but there was no more anger or bitterness. The point is that they were two different people, and in the end, they simply drifted apart. Elaine wanted kids and a house with a white picket fence, two dogs, and an SUV, with a husband that worked nine to five. He couldn't give her that, not at the time anyway. So, as a result, she went out and found what she wanted. He was happy for her, he truly was, but he promised himself that he would never marry again and committed himself to the fact that he would focus on work and God.

"Morning Jarod," Pastor Rossouw greeted as he unlocked the church.

"Morning Pastor, lovely day today, isn't it?"

"Indeed, we need the rain; hopefully it's here to stay for a few days."

The unexpected gift of rain had been a blessing after weeks of drought and unbearable heat, and although the rainy season was still a few weeks ago, the skies didn't lie. Jarod loved the rain.

"According to the weather, we can expect rainfall for at least three days," he chuckled and then entered the church and waited for the pastor to turn the lights on.

"Are you going to move up a pew?" Pastor Rossouw asked.

Jarod shook his head and smiled, "Maybe next time."

The pastor didn't push him, but he always asked him out of interest more than anything, that was the extent of their conversations. More small talk really. The pastor went on about his business and Jarod took a seat in his usual spot, waiting patiently for the pews to fill up.

Today, however, with the rain falling, he didn't expect the church to be packed. He always found it rather odd how people would run about in the rain to get to Walmart or go places, but the moment it rains they use it as an excuse to skip church.

One by one individual and families arrived, filling the pews from the front of the church towards the back. Two youngsters came bolting down the side aisle and darted between a couple talking in the front, then they disappeared under the pews. No one seemed to be perturbed by their playfulness, which he liked. Then again the sign right above the small stage read – Let the little children come to me, and do not hinder them.

He turned his attention back to the small hymnal in his hands, and paged aimlessly through it, trying to appear preoccupied, in the hope that no-one tried to make any conversation with him. But his hopes were dashed with Pastor Rossouw spoke next to him.

"Jarod, I would like you to meet Christine, my daughter."

Jarod stood up and wiped his hand on the back of his jeans and then extended it to the woman in front of him. She was beautiful, tall with long blond hair that flowed loosely over her shoulders. But the smile that tugged at the corner of her lips didn't reach her light blue eyes. It was as if the lights were on but nobody was home, she was just going through the motions.

"It's a pleasure to meet you, Christine," he said and shook her hand firmly.

"It's a pleasure," she repeated his words and removed her hand.

"Jarod is a firefighter, I thought you two would have a lot in common," Pastor Rossouw piped up and Jarod wanted to shrink away, but he remained poised.

"You're also in the department?" he asked out of interest.

"Not exactly, I'm in forensics, I investigate the aftermath and the cause of the fire," she answered.

"Nice," he said, not sure what else to add.

He felt awkward with her, not in a negative kind of way, but purely because he hasn't spoken to a woman on a casual basis since before he was married. And when the pastor walked away leaving the two of them alone in each other's company, he shrugged and stepped back.

"You can sit here if you want?" he offered.

This time she smiled, "I won't mind at all, anything but sitting right in the front where my dad wants me."

Jarod chuckled and moved over two spaces, leaving enough space between them. They sat in silence for a while before Christine spoke.

"You have to excuse my dad, he can be very forward at times," she smiled, "He keeps wanting to set me up for dates."

Jarod laughed at that, "Playing pastor and matchmaker, I see."

She rolled her eyes, "Yeah, he does it every time I set foot in a church, which is why I'm never here," she turned to look at him, "I haven't seen you here before, though."

He shrugged, "I've been here a few months now, but I don't stay around to mingle with the members. I just come for my daily bread and then I disappear."

"Ah, I see," she said, "The dash and go type."

"Yeah, that would be me."

"You do know that church is meant for communion and encouragement from fellow Christians."

He leaned forward with his elbows on his knees and regarded the congregation, "I come here to learn and find peace."

"A man with depth, well I'm sure you'll find peace being stuck here in the back all the time."

"It's worked so far."

Throughout the service, Jarod was acutely aware of the woman who was seated next to him. The aroma of her perfume kept wafting past him, making him shift uncomfortably in his seat. By the time the service came to an end, he couldn't wait to get out. He needed fresh air and fast.

"Well Jarod, it was a nice having company here at the back," Christine said as she stood up to let him pass.

"Yeah, it was," he dragged his hand over his stubbly short hair, "I'll see you around?"

All she did was nod, and that was his queue. He exited this church like a bolt of lightning.

Chapter 3

Christine did not expect that at all. She knew her father was up to something when he insisted on her coming to church. She was prepared for the worst, him introducing her to another pastor, or one of the deacons, or worst case, preaching hellfire and brimstone to try and get her to get back into the habit of going to church. The last thing she expected was to be introduced to a firefighter. And not just any firefighter, Jarod Marks had all the bits and pieces that would make any woman turn into a fan-girl. He was built like an MMA fighter, he had deep willow green eyes and brown, almost black hair that was neatly trimmed and on top of that, he had that five o'clock shadow that danced across his chin, making him look even manlier than he possibly could. For the first time in years, she wondered if her anti-dating motto was even viable. Just because she made one bad choice in life, by dating Darryl, didn't mean that every man she met would be like him.

After the service, she had spoken to her dad and tried to find out more about Jarod, of course, her dad was all too happy to tell her that he's a firefighter, with a deep soul, but beyond that, he didn't want to divulge any personal information. He did, however, mention that Jarod had also been in a bad relationship that left him weary of dating, much like her.

So what if he was damaged goods, she, though, he couldn't possibly be more damaged than she was.

Thankfully thinking about Jarod and the possibility of entering the dating scene again was a momentarily lapse in judgment, but the next day, she had once again gotten her mind focused on work and making sure she didn't fall into the dating trap again. Or so she thought. Every now and again, when she wasn't going through case files or looking at labs of fire starters that contained possible chemicals, Jarod's face floated into her mind. It got to a point where she went for her second visit to the cafeteria in one week, which was totally out of character. This time she opted for a slice of cheesecake and strong coffee.

"Rossouw!" one of her colleagues called. "Having a love affair with that cheesecake?"

"Shut it, Kemp," she mumbled and took a generous scoop out of spite and shoved it all into her mouth.

Dalton Kemp came over and pulled the chair out, plonking himself down, "You really need to get out more, we're having a get-together tonight at Franks' are you coming around?"

Franks was a bar not too far from the office, where they staff often went to wind down after a rough day at the office. Most of the time she opted out of going to mingle, but tonight was an exception, she needed a distraction.

"Yeah sure, I'll see you there at around seven."

"Great, bring your date," Kemp chuckled and dug her coffee spoon into her cheesecake.

"Hey! Stop that," she muttered and pulled her plate away.

One thing about her line of work and the people she worked with was that they were all like family. And this was the only family where she felt she belonged. Back at home, with her mom and dad, she felt like the odd one out, simply because she didn't share in their beliefs. She used to, but it all changed in her first year of being a firefighter. It was during that year, where she realized that God helps who he wants to. She had seen too many tragic deaths that included young children and elderly people to think that there was anything merciful about God. After a year of being a firefighter, she eventually opted to take a job in forensics and fire investigations and was transferred. Now instead of running into burning buildings to save people, she now investigated the aftermath instead.

At around noon, after her last case file was concluded, she locked her office and made her way to Franks' to join the others. The atmosphere was festive and the place was crowded. She spotted her colleagues at the far end near the back of the pup and wrangled her way through the crowd.

"Rossouw! You made it, where's Mr. Cheesecake?" Kemp called out raising his beer to her.

She rolled her eyes and laughed, "We had a fight, I left him in the cafeteria to bond with Miss Caramel," she joked.

She ordered herself a cola since she wasn't really one for drinking and joined the rest. The mood was light, and no one spoke about work, which was a relief. She opted for a seat at the far end of the table next to Janet, the receptionist, who was a gray little mouse who barely spoke as it was. She was a bit of an introvert, so other than sipping on her drink she didn't add much value to the conversation. But Christine didn't mind that at all.

It was a while later when a sudden explosion ripped through the kitchen and an orange flame punched its way into the main bar area. Windows shattered and people fell to the ground as smoke and fire billowed into the establishment. Caroline grabbed Jannet and pulled her down to the ground almost instantly as panic erupted. Everywhere people were trying to make it out of the bar, some managing just before the flames engulfed the front entrance.

"Bathroom!" Christine cried out as she tugged Janet's arm, practically dragging her along the side of the wall towards the back where the restrooms were. With any luck they could find a way out through one of the small windows, worst cases they would have water.

The fire alarms erupted over and above the agonizing cries of everyone stuck in the building and Christine knew that if they made it out of here alive, it would be a miracle. Her hope to find an escape route through one of the smaller windows was futile, she might fit through one at a squeeze but Janet won't and she refused to leave the young girl behind. Huddled in the corner of the bathroom, with her arms wrapped around the frantic girl, she could only hope that someone will get to them in time. For the first time in years, she prayed for help.

Christine thought fast, she pulled off her top and drenched it with water, then handed it to Janet, "Here, keep this over your mouth and nose, try to take shallow breaths okay?"

She then grabbed her denim jacket and did the same. Smoke was starting to fill the bathroom and the heat from the main room was slowly pushing towards the back. Time was of the essence, and if the fire department did not arrive soon, they would all meet their maker.

"We're going to die!" Janet panicked.

"No we're not, help is on its way," Christine shouted over the noise of crackling flames and falling banisters.

The sound of approaching sirens was a relief to some extent, at least the fire department was here, but the question that plagued her, was if they would get to them in time. Christine assessed their situation. The fire hadn't reached the restrooms yet, but the heat was excruciating, and smoke pummeled into the small room stealing all the oxygen. She instructed Janet to stay put while she crawled out from under the sink, keeping her body bowed low on the ground. She needed to get to one of the windows and call for help. She felt her way around the floor until she reached one of the cubicles, and then she clambered her way to the window.

"Help! We're in here!" she shouted between bouts of coughs and heaving for air. Her throat was burning and her lungs were filled with smoke, but she refused to give up, "Help!" she called again and again.

"Over here!" she heard someone shout and only then did she allow herself to collapse on the floor. At least now someone would try to get to them.

The last thing she remembered was the incessant smoke that filled the room and the unbearable heat that licked at her skin before her entire world went black.

"Christine! Stay with me!" she recognized the voice from somewhere but she couldn't quite place it, "Christine can you hear me?"

She tried to respond but she simply couldn't. Her brain was doing all the work but the signal to the rest of her body was down. She kept drifting in and out of consciousness but the cool air that surrounded her meant that she was no longer in the inferno. That, or she had died and gone to, wherever bad girls go.

"Where is the ambulance!" she heard her savior call out.

"J... Janet," she managed to utter.

"She's responsive! Christine, it's Jarod, you've had some smoke inhalation, do you know where you are?" she heard him asked.

She tried to open her eyes, but it felt like a million cinders were stuck to her eyeballs, "Where is Janet," she asked first and foremost.

"She's fine, she's alive, thanks to you," he said and squeezed her hand, "But now we need to take care of you."

"Jarod?" she asked half deliriously, "From church?"

He chuckled and brushed her hair from her face, "Yeah Jarod from church, now save your breath. The ambulance will take you to the hospital; I'll come by later to check up on you."

She reached blindly for his hand and squeezed it, "Thank you," she whispered as her head spun and she once again plummeted into a dark hole.

Chapter 4

Jarod was the first to arrive at the hospital, followed by Christine's mom and dad, who both looked like they had been crying.

"Pastor Rossouw..." Jarod started.

"Call me James," he said to Jarod and then introduced his wife, "This is Marjorie, have you heard anything?"

He shook his head, "No I haven't, I'm not family but I know that she had inhaled a lot of smoke, but thankfully the fire never reached them."

"Oh thank you, Lord," her mother exclaimed casting her eyes to the heavens.

"Christine was very brave," Jarod said as he told the couple how she burrowed into the restrooms with her colleague, using very basic methods to keep from suffocating, "When she decided to call for help, was when she inhaled most of the smoke. But if she hadn't done that, no one would have known they were in the bathroom."

Marjorie sat down and cupped her hand over her mouth and James sat down beside her, wrapping his arm around her shoulders, "You were heaven sent," he said to Jarod, "Thank you for saving our little girl."

Jarod smiled and shook his head, "I was just doing my duty sir Pastor."

He left the couple and made his way down the corridor to get some coffee, he was still in uniform, covered in soot and smelling like a furnace, but he didn't want to go until he was a hundred percent sure that Christine was out of danger.

A while later he returned and made his way to where Christine's room was, through the window he saw the Pastor and his wife talking to Christine, who looked like hell but beautiful all the same. She was alive, and by the looks of it, recovering. Thankfully she didn't sustain any burns, it could have been so much worse.

Christine had spotted him just as he was about to leave and waved him over. When he entered the room, her mom and dad excused themselves to go get a bite to eat.

"How are you feeling?" he asked as he pulled a chair closer.

"Like a pizza base right out of the oven?" she said and laughed, but then coughed and clutched her chest, "change that, I feel like I've been to hell and back."

Jarod chuckled and handed her a glass of water, "It was quite something you did back there, your dad mentioned to me you were a firefighter before."

She took a sip of water and counted her breaths, "Yeah, for a year, then I moved to fire forensics."

"I'm glad you didn't forget the training then, it came in handy," he commented.

Even as she lay there, pale as a sheet, with her blond hair still covered in soot and ash, she was beautiful. He never thought that he would even look at another woman after his wife cheated on him, and here he was, doing just that.

He cleared his throat and made an effort to leave, but Christine caught his arm, and smiled, "I owe you dinner and a movie," she said half smiling.

He chuckled and nodded, "As soon as you're back on your feet, I'll come to collect."

Soon he was ushered away when the nurses entered to do the general BP checks, but for a moment he stood looking at her over their heads.

"And the Lord God said, It is not good that a man should be alone," a disembodied voice sounded and Jarod turned to respond, but there was no one else around, other than the nurses going about their business.

Puzzled he turned and looked back at Christine and then waved and left. This was the strangest thing he had ever experienced. It was as if there was someone else there with him, someone far more enlightened than he was. But the words stuck to him all the way home. And he realized beyond a shadow of a doubt that Christine did not appear in his life out of mere coincidence. This was something far bigger than him, or anyone else for that matter.

Chapter 5

Within a few days, Christine was discharged from hospital and sent home to recover. On her mother's insistence, she had no choice but to spend another week staying her folks until she was strong enough to return to work, but every day, Jarod made an effort to visit her, and if he couldn't get to her physically, he would call her. At first, she thought nothing of it, assuming that he was simply being nice, but out of the blue, every time her phone rang and his caller ID flickered on her screen, her stomach would rumble with excitement. Or when she heard his car pull up, she could hardly contain herself. Her dad, of course, wasn't blind either. He knew exactly what was going on.

"Jarod's a fine young man," he said one morning over coffee.

"Yeah, he's nice," she mumbled into her cup.

"Do you like him?"

She whipped her head around and looked at her dad, but the way he smiled at her disarmed her completely and she felt a blush creep into her cheeks, "Yeah, a little."

Her dad chuckled, and Christine put her cup down, "How do you know when you meet the right person?" she asked.

Her dad took his reading glasses off and regarded her, "That's a tough one on answer sweetheart, but sometimes you just know."

She worried her lip and looked into the distance. She had spent all this time guarding her own heart against heartbreak and disappointment. For so long she refused to believe that love existed and convinced herself that she didn't need anyone to go home too. But tragedy has a way to open one's eyes and this is exactly what happened to her. While she was trapped in that restroom practically staring death in the face, her first instinct was to pray and ask God to help her and Janet out of that pickle. It was at that point where she remembered to use what she had to her advantage. And not once during that entire time while they were stuck in that room did she panic, it was an ethereal calm that had taken over and now that she has had time to think it over, she could only come to one conclusion. God had sent His angels to help them. And she was convinced that Jarod was one of them, her personal angel. The thought of him warmed up her heart and a smile spread across her face.

"Penny for your thoughts?" her dad asked.

"I think it's time I go back to church," she said, "and I think I want to give love a chance."

Her dad put his book down and turned to her, smiling, "It's only when you leap into the water that you learn to swim sweetheart. Trust in the Lord and he will make a way clear for you."

Her dad always had wise comebacks, and although she still had a lot to overcome, she knew that little baby steps would eventually get her there.

At around noon, Jared's car rumbled outside, and Christine gave herself one last once-over in the mirror. It was date night, and she was nervous. She tucked a stray strand of hair back into place pulled her lips into a tight pout and released it. It felt as if the muscles in her face were refusing to cooperate.

"Honey!" her mom called and she took a deep steadying breath before making her way to the living room.

When she saw Jared, her heart did that familiar tumble, "Hi," she said and mentally rolled her eyes at her own silliness, "I mean, welcome?" she shook her head, "Never mind, are you ready to go?"

Jared chuckled and nodded at her dad and her mom, "We won't be out very late," he said and Christine literally dragged him out of the house.

"Are you okay?" he asked with a hint of humor in his voice.

"Do I look okay?" she chirped.

"You look fine to me."

Her internal thermometer was about to pop. The way he looked at her when he said she looked fine made her feel all warm and fuzzy inside. She reminded herself that she wasn't a teenager on a first date and forced to compose herself.

"I'm sorry, I just, I haven't been on a date in ages," she said as he opened the passenger door for her.

"Well that makes two of us, so trust me, there's no need to be nervous."

That was a relief she thought, but still, her heart kept thrumming against her chest.

Jarod had surprised her with a visit to a local musical arts theater, where they were hosting a fundraiser for a little girl who needed a skin graph after having sustained serious burns when she was caught in a burning car. Again, he had completely swept her feet out from under her, and she was in complete awe by how passionate he was.

"So do you always get involved in these fundraisers?" she asked curiously over dessert.

He chuckled and reached to wipe a smudge of cream from her chin, "Not always, it depends on the nature of the campaign. Sarah has a special place in my heart, she was only four when the car they were traveling in was involved in a head-on collision. Besides the fact that she was trapped in the burning car, she lost both her parents."

Christine swallowed at the lump in her throat, "That's terrible; I can't even begin to imagine how hard that must be for her."

This was exactly what she couldn't understand, why God would allow such a thing to happen, was just too cruel to comprehend.

"There's actually more to the story than most would believe," he said quietly, "You see, her parents were both alcoholics, and there were a few cases of child abuse against them, but the system failed her. But the funny thing is, after the accident, the driver of the other car, who survived, decided to adopt her and they are paying for all her medical bills."

Christine's jaw dropped and she blinked at the tears that threatened to spill.

"That's nothing short of a miracle," she said softly.

"You can say that again. It's true, God works in mysterious ways, and we don't always know the answers, but He does."

She was both shocked and thrilled by the news, and she couldn't help but cry. Jarod shifted his chair closer to hers and wrapped his arm around her shoulder.

"I didn't mean to make you cry, this is supposed to be the first date," he whispered.

"You didn't make me cry, it's just that," she sniffed against his shoulder, "all this time I figured God was merciless, never once did I consider a bigger picture."

"Shhh," Jarod comforted her and held her close, "It sometimes takes an extraordinary event to make us see things through His eyes, and all I know is that God never fails us, it's only our own expectations."

Chapter 6

Christine took a deep steadying breath as she stood at the end of the aisle, her dad by her side, and Jarod waiting in front, wearing his step out fireman's uniform with all his decorated medals. To the left were all his mates, and the entire squadron of firefighters some wearing their uniforms, other also wearing step outs, to the right was her family and some of her colleagues.

Her big day had arrived; she was finally going to promise herself to the one man she was willing to trust with her life. The wedding march started and she counted her steps in her mind, like a waltz down the aisle.

"I'm so proud to be your father," her dad whispered without moving his lips.

"Daddy you make me proud," she said, "thank you for introducing me to Jared."

Her insides were a kaleidoscope of butterflies and as her father handed her over to her future husband, she couldn't her fingers from trembling, but Jared took her hands in his and smiled at her. His eyes mirrored the same love she felt, and instantly he calmed her down.

It was a day to remember, Christine had not only promised herself to the love of her life, she also found God somewhere in the mix. Somewhere along the line, she realized that God never left; all she had to do was turn around and call on Him.

Christine and Jared lived happily ever after, doing what they both loved and in each other, they found the missing puzzle pieces that made them both complete.

"Are we going to go for green or yellow?" Christine asked holding up two cans of paint.

"Why not do both," Jared said as he worked at assembling the crib.

"Mmm, good point," she said and placed the two small tins on the coffee table, "how is the crib coming along?"

Jared stood up discarding the spanner and pulled his pregnant wife into his arms, "I think we just get our baby to share our bed for a while," he chuckled.

Christine laughed and wrapped her arms around her husband's neck, "I love you," she murmured against his lips.

"And I love you, Christine Marks," Jared said and kissed her.

ANGELA'S CHURCH

KORI HOUSTON

Chapter One

Angela packed away the last of her belongings, holding up a crystal vase that had belonged to her mother.

"Please be careful with that," she begged but her words fell on deaf ears as the man roughly grabbed the vase and dumped it into a carton filled with more of Angela's things. She dabbed at her eyes with a wad of tissue and then turned away, unable to bear witness to the horrible sight of her childhood home being robbed of everything that she and her parents had worked so hard to build together.

"Angie, it's your dad," her friend Clara held out her phone.

"Hi Daddy,"Angela said faking a cheerful voice as she took the phone.

She could hear the cough lingering in his voice as he asked her how it was going.

"Oh, it's all good- we're just waiting for them to pack all the boxes into the van. I'll be done here in about half an hour."

There was a brief pause on the other end.

"Half an hour- that's all it'll take to pack up our life in that house. I'll see you soon, darling."

Angela handed the phone back to Clara who shook her head and hugged her.

"It'll be alright, I promise. I'll stay here and get this sorted out, why don't you head over to your new apartment and set it up, hmm?" Clara said affectionately.

Angela nodded, picking up the two boxes which held all the items she had been allowed to keep since they had no resale value. She hailed a cab and read her new address off a scrap of paper. As she sat in the back of the cab with its strange smells and sticky seats, she desperately missed her chauffeur-driven luxury car. She sighed and looked out the window- she could no longer afford to live her old life, and she needed to readjust her standards if she desired any chance of being happy. She was more worried about her father, who had suffered a near-fatal heart attack the moment he had heard the news of his business partner's betrayal.

Decades of hard work, and millions of dollars were lost in the blink of an eye. The bank had seized everything, their house, their things- not even Angela's clothes in her closet were hers anymore; everything belonged to the bank. She was trying to push through it all with a smile on her face, but it was becoming increasingly harder and harder. Her father had been a real-estate mogul for as long as she could remember, and Angela had never wanted for anything growing up. Now, twenty-three years later, here she was, with no money and a very ick father to take care of.

"Here we are," the cab driver called out, and Angela looked up to see the seediest, most damaged building she had ever seen.

"No- that can't be right," she said mostly to herself, but the cabbie shook his head.

"Nope, this is it."

Angela held back her tears and nodded solemnly, rummaging in her wallet for enough money to pay the cab fare.

She carried her boxes over to the shanty building with its peeling paint and overflowing dumpsters, and she whispered a quick prayer, reminding herself that God was just testing her, and that it was all for the better. She took a deep breath and walked inside, where she saw a bored security guard lazily inspecting his nails.

"Excuse me," she said brightly, and the man looked up with an air of apathy.

"Yes?"

Angela set down the boxes and extended her hand but the guard merely looked at it until she withdrew it.

"I'm Angela Wolfe, and I'm renting out apartment 403."

"And?"the guard raised an eyebrow.

"And- hello? Angela licked her lips."That's all I wanted to say really- just introduce myself, that's all."

"Well, you did that."

"Yes- yes I did. Anyway, see you around."

She picked up the boxes and walked towards the elevator when she heard the guard call out.

"It's out of order."

She looked up and saw a notice hanging on the wall, yellowing with age.

"Oh, right. Okay, I'll just take the stairs then."

Once Angela had managed to lug the two boxes up four flights of stairs, she stood outside apartment 403, and took another deep breath.

"Okay," she said to herself, "Moment of truth."

She unlocked the door with the keys she had been given and pushed it open. She was instantly hit with a smell so vile she couldn't describe it, and she covered her nose as she glanced around at the dust-covered rugs and furniture, and the single naked light bulb that hung from the ceiling in the center of what appeared to be the living room. Angela dragged the boxes inside and placed her hands on her hips, resisting the urge to gag from the smell as she looked around.

"Alright- new DIY project. It'll be okay," she said brightly, but her voice cracked at the last word and she knew it wasn't alright- it was far from alright. When she had imagined living in a small rented apartment, she had imagined a cute little terrace where she could place some succulents in cute white planters and a cozy coffee table where she could call her friends and serve them wine and cheese. As she looked around now, she realized she could never invite anybody over. Her old life was gone, and she had to accept it now. She shook her head, and walked out of the apartment, again- it was making her miserable after just five minutes of being in there. She decided to go see her father, even if it meant putting on a performance like she always had to- pretending everything was fine and cheery when they both knew it wasn't.

Chapter Two

She played with her pearls as she sat in the waiting room, the only reminder now of a life she had once led. Her father hadn't let her sell those, and she was glad- they were all she had left of her mother and now they were her only link to the past.

"Miss Wolfe?" The receptionist called out. "Your father's awake- you can go see him now."

Angela looked up, startled out of her thoughts. She thanked the receptionist and made her way to her father's private room- thank goodness for health insurance, or they wouldn't even be able to afford the hospital fees.

"Sweetie," her father said sleepily, "I didn't expect to see you here, weren't you supposed to move into your new place today?"

"Yes, but I missed you too much, so here I am," she said as she gently laid a hand across his forehead.

"Well I'm glad for the company- how's the apartment?"

Her father smiled as he sat up and put on his glasses, For a second, Angela considered breaking down in front of her father but she held it together and smiled.

"Oh, it's just lovely- very cozy and um- quaint."

"Quaint?"her father raised an eyebrow.

"Oh you know, it's very old fashioned- I can spruce it up with a nice rug or two, maybe a lamp," she replied, nodding enthusiastically.

"Angie- if you don't like it, we can set you up somewhere else. What about Clara? I'm sure you can spend some time with her."

"No, no it's a lovely place, don't worry. And I wouldn't want to burden Clara anyway, she's getting married in two months and I would just be in the way,"she said.

"Daddy- please you have to rest!"Angela said hurrying over to him as he tried to get up but he grimaced with pain and fell back into bed.

"Fetch me that file, would you?" he nodded and pointed to a table in the corner

"What's that?"

Angela picked up the clear folder and handed it to him.

"It just might be our salvation." He pulled out a sheaf of paper.

"Yes- just as I had hoped, it's not in the company's name."

"What's not in the company's name?" she inquired curiously – craning her neck trying to glance at the paper but it was too far away.

"Angie, there's an old property on the edge of town- I acquired it very early on, before we established Wolfe-Moore Industries, and if we restore it and sell it, we can earn a pretty good sum from it," he said gravely as he sat up again and took off his glasses. He handed her the document.

"But it has to be you- only you can handle the property."

As Angela pored over the sheet, she realized why it had to be her- the name on the deed was her mother's, and according to her mother's will, Angela had inherited all her property.

"So this property- it belongs to me?" She asked uncertainly and her father nodded.

"Daddy, it's too much. We've lost everything, can't you see that? This one little house isn't going to change anything, no matter who buys it, and why would anyone purchase anything from us anyway? We're bankrupt, the whole company's been exposed in all of the newspapers; everyone knows we haven't got two cents to rub together. I walked here, Daddy, because I didn't have enough to pay the cab driver- can you believe that? I walked here my horrible rat-infested building to this hospital which is like ten blocks, but I didn't have a choice because we're poor," she said in an unexpected fit of rage.

After she was done, she held onto the bedpost to stop herself from swaying.

"I'm sorry," she said meekly. But to her surprise, her father laughed.

"You look just like your mother when you get angry- she also yelled at me like that quite often."

Angela crossed her arms over her chest, and smiled reluctantly.

"So I was right- you don't like your apartment?" he added.

Angela shrugged and said,

"No- it's alright. I mean- yeah I hate it. It's terrible, Daddy- it smells so bad and I think there might be a small animal living in there," she said shrugging her shoulders.

He laughed again and she smiled, it was good to hear him laugh after all this time.

"That's why I'm so keen on restoring this property, Angie. It's a good one I promise, and once you work your magic on it, it will make things a lot easier for us."

"You're not gonna let this go, are you? Always a businessman- even from the hospital bed," she shook her head and sighed.

"So you'll do it?"

"Yes, I'll do it- like I could have ever said no to you anyway. So what is this property anyway?"

"It's beautiful, Angela, it's just a stunning structure- The Trinity Church," he answered beaming widely.

Chapter Three

Angela climbed out of the car and gazed up in awe of the beautiful structure. It was a huge gothic church, complete with its pointed arches and ribbed vaults. Clara climbed out beside her and stood with her as the two gazed on silently, stunned speechless by the church's majesty. As they looked on, however, they realized the church was actually falling apart.

The flying buttresses were crumbling, threatening to collapse any second, and Angela instinctively knew that her father was right- saving this church meant saving their family. Clara patted her gently on the shoulder and Angela smiled.

"Shall we go inside?" Angela asked Clara.

"Oh please- let's."

The two women took deep breaths and walked purposefully towards the giant doors of the church. They were heavy and needed their combined strength to push them open. Clara immediately started coughing as the dust swirled inside and Angela looked around, fascinated but dismayed at the amount of work that would be needed.

She was unusually quiet on the drive back, and listened silently as Clara went on and on, about the church and the country club and her fiancé.

"Angie!"

"Sorry- I was thinking about the church. Clara, I'll need to hire someone; a contactor. But I don't have any money," she was startled out of her thoughts.

Clara frowned as she thought about it.

"Oh I know! You know David volunteers at our church whenever he can-" she said brightly as she got a brainwave.

"Oh God, Clara- can you stop talking about your fiancé and help me out?"

Clara shot Angela a withering look and continued on.

"As I was saying, *David* works with some men who are recovering addicts trying to find their way back to God, and they're being given some vocational training. I'll ask him if there are any construction workers or contractors he could send your way. They charge very little, so it shouldn't be a problem."

Angela suddenly felt terrible about snapping at her best friend, but before she could even apologize, Clara waved a hand dismissively.

"Don't worry about it. I know you're stressed. Okay, so where should I drop you, the hospital or your apartment?"

"The hospital please," Angela said quickly, not wanting to show Clara where she lived just yet.

As they pulled up to the hospital, Angela thanked Clara and quickly hurried off, so her friend wouldn't ask her too many questions or guess that she was trying to hide something.

She walked quickly to her father's room but slowed down as she neared the door to his ward. She often had to prepare herself before she walked in- it was always so hard to see her father like that. Angela's mother had passed away when she was ten years old, and for the next fourteen years, she had seen her father as her pillar of strength. Too see him lying in a hospital bed connected to tubes and machines was always very difficult for her.

"Hi Daddy," she called out when she walked in. He lowered the book he was reading and smiled.

"Hi sweetheart, I didn't expect to see you today. Weren't you going to go see the church?"

"Mmhmm, I did go. It's a beautiful old church, but it's a lot of work," she said nodding and peering at the book cover.

Her father tried to sit up but Angela looked at him sternly and he lay back down with a sigh.

"I know, I know- it's crumbling but it would be such a shame to let it go to waste. Come on, tell me what you really thought."

"It really is gorgeous- and the architecture is just exquisite. I mean the arches, and I think I saw the remains of a stained-glass window. Truly stunning, I can see why you held onto it for so long," she accepted with a smile.

Her father didn't say anything, but when Angela looked at him, he had tears in his eyes.

"Dad, what's wrong?"

"Your mother loved that old church. She was always telling me to work on it but I was so busy with other things, things I thought more profitable-"

"Maybe this was fate. Maybe it was meant to be this way- that I would restore it for her."

Her father held her hand to his heart and then wept softly, and Angela tried very hard to fight back her own tears, but in vain.

When the nurse walked in a minute later, she was startled and ashamed of intruding on them.

"I'll come back later," she mumbled and left.

"No- please, you go ahead. I have to run anyway," she kissed the top of her father's balding head and said, "Bye Daddy."

She hurried out of the room before he could say anything and when she was outside, she leaned against the wall for a few minutes trying to put herself together again. Somehow, speaking about her mother always made her emotional, even after all this time had passed. Being in the hospital reminded her of the time when her mother was sick and it brought back the terrible feeling of loss and the fear of losing a parent.

Once she had managed to collect herself, she walked out of the hospital and got a cab to take her to the new apartment. As she walked up the dirty stairwell, she felt like breaking down- everything in her life was so overwhelmingly difficult all at once and she didn't know if she would be able to make it. For the first time in a long time, she stopped where she was and pressed her palms together as she began to pray.

A few people passed her by on the stairs, but Angela continued to pray until she felt better, and then she slowly continued up the stairs, reaching her apartment and taking a deep breath. "I can do this," she said to herself, and pushed the door open.

The same dust and smell rose to greet her, but this time, she was determined to stop feeling miserable and do something about it. She walked straight towards the kitchen and picked up the cleaning supplies she had bought earlier that day.

"Alright," she said looking around, not knowing where to start, "Let's clean this mess."

Chapter Four

Angela had started to pick her way through the dusty pews when she heard the car pull up. Excitedly, she turned back and walked to the large double doors. As she neared the entrance, a tall man walked through- he was lanky and thin and had the air of someone who had lost a lot of weight all at once and far too quickly. He smiled pleasantly and held his hand out.

"Hello- you must be Angela. I'm Nathan, nice to meet you."

Angela shook his hand and greeted him warmly, showing him into the church as though she were welcoming a guest into her home.

"So this place really is something, huh?" he said looking around – letting out a low whistle.

"Nothing a little bit of love and care won't fix," she said confidently.

"No, I mean look at it- it's beautiful."

Angela was surprised to see someone like him stand so in awe of a church and she quickly reminded herself not to judge a book by its cover- even of the cover looked shabby and dog-eared.

That's what Nathan looked like- as though he was worn out with time and usage, his young body ageing rapidly as his muscles atrophied. There was a slight revulsion that Angela felt and she tried very hard to control it as she showed him around. He seemed enthusiastic about the work though and Angela was glad about that.

"You know, that window could be re-painted, the pews can be polished, and I can take a look at the buttressed right away, they seem to be weakening with age." He was talking fast and Angela nodded quickly, feeling much more reassured about him and his abilities.

"Excellent, yes we can start right away if you like. I'll have a contract drawn up tomorrow so that we discuss your salary-" but he didn't let her finish as he waved a hand dismissively.

"No no, I'm just looking for work, but I don't need to be paid. Especially for a project like this- it's so meaningful."

Angela bristled for a moment as she thought that Clara might have told David why this church was so important to Angela, and David might have told Nathan, but then she quickly realized that Nathan had simply meant that it was meaningful because it was a church. She also remembered what Clara had told her about Nathan trying to find his way back to God.

"Are you sure you don't want me to pay you? I mean you can't work for free."

"No, for this kind of project I could enter ask for payment. This is God's work, and if I'm successful I will owe it all to you and to Him," he said shaking his head.

Angela stood in awe of him and suddenly felt terrible for thinking the worst of him when she first saw him.

"I- This church means a lot to me," Angela said, and she expected him to ask her why.

"Well then I want to make sure that I do a good job," he replied acting indifferent to its backstory.

Angela watched him as he walked around the church, inspecting things and talking to himself, she felt a strange feeling that she could not describe. She shook her head and focused on the task ahead, ignoring the sensation in her belly and joining Nathan in examining the walls and frescoes.

"This is gorgeous work- but I'm worried there might be mold lurking around somewhere. It's a difficult job for sure- do you mind if I bring a team of my men with me to help out?"

Angela blinked- the thought of having strange men surround her in an abandoned church should have caused her to panic, but instead she found herself nodding.

"Yeah- that's great, we should be done sooner then."

Nathan smiled and continued, and even though Angela followed him, she wasn't listening to what he was saying. Instead, she looked at him- really looked. He had a tall, thin frame but he was surprisingly strong and could lift things out of the way very easily, his clothes were old but neatly pressed and mended in some places, and they were far too big for him. He had light brown hair that was swept back from his face and green eyes that were so large they looked almost out of place on his thin face.

At one point, Nathan saw him looking at her and smiled, catching Angela off guard. She turned red and fluttered her eyelashes embarrassedly, quickly pretending to be looking at the stained glass work on the windows instead, and letting her long black hair fall forwards to cover her face.

She was trying to be quiet as a mouse so she wouldn't draw attention to herself just now, and suddenly, her phone started to ring. She leapt up, startled, and pulled her phone out of her pocket.

"Hey Clara," she said into the phone with a sigh.

"Angie- how's everything? Did the contractor get there?"

Angela dropped her voice and edged towards the door.

"Yes, he's here. He seems like he knows what he's doing, so tell David thanks please," she whispered into the phone.

"It's Nathan right? He's really wonderful, and he's very hard-working, but if he gives you any trouble, just tell David, okay?"

Angle thanked her friend and hung up, turning around and gasping when she found Nathan inches away from her.

"Sorry, I didn't mean to creep up on you," he said, blinking at her with those strange green eyes of his, "But I'm done with the notes and calculations. I can go back and get the materials now- would you like me to drop you home on the way?"

Angela nodded, not wishing to be stranded out here trying to catch a cab, but still not comfortable with letting people know where she lived. She glanced at him as they walked out of the church, and wondered where he lived- would he judge her building and apartment if he saw it? Did he live in worse conditions? She shook her head slightly, feeling terrible for assuming that he lived in poverty.

She climbed into the passenger seat and looked out of the window, smiling slightly at Nathan as he climbed in from the other side and revved the engine.

Chapter Five

As they neared her building, Angela considered asking him to drop her off somewhere else like a supermarket, but she stayed quiet and let him drive on.

"It's the next left, right?" Nathan asked when they were almost there.

Angela nodded, waiting for it to be over.

"Here we are," he said as he pulled up and passed her a smile.

She suddenly felt a lot more at ease- he hadn't reacted at all.

"Would you like to come upstairs? I can make some coffee," she asked spontaneously.

Nathan's expression changed to one of wonder, and Angela worried that she may have made a mistake.

"I'd love to. I haven't had a good cup of coffee in days," he replied cheerfully.

Angela led him upstairs and he followed quietly until they reached her apartment. She considered warning him that it wasn't entirely clean yet, but she didn't. Instead, she pushed open the door and welcomed him in. He smiled as he stepped inside; looking around as he nervously wrung his hands together. Angela looked around too- she had cleaned up a little bit, and the dust was all gone, replaced by some rugs from the old house and two small armchairs. She had put small planters on the windowsill to hide the ugly view of the neighbor's clotheslines. She anxiously waited for Nathan to say something, but he didn't, and she was glad.

"Why don't you take a seat," she said gesturing to the armchairs, "And I'll make us some coffee?"

Nathan hesitantly sat down, still fidgeting nervously, and Angela went off to the kitchen, pulling out mugs as she thought about the fact that there was a strange man in her house. She had only known Nathan for a few hours but somehow, she felt comfortable enough around him to know that she needn't worry. She heaped a spoonful or two of coffee powder into mugs and added sugar and cream, before carrying it out in a small tray.

"Sorry, I only have instant coffee- I hope that's alright," she said, setting the tray down and handing him a mug.

"No, that's perfect- thank you," he said taking the warm mug in both hands.

She was settling into the other armchair when her phone began to ring.

"Sorry," she muttered fishing it out her pocket and answering it.

"Miss Wolfe?" A voice urgently said on the other line, "It's Nurse Farris from the hospital- I'm afraid your father's had another heart attack. The doctors are seeing to him now and he's under care but I suggest you come down here quickly."

Angela nearly dropped the phone and without a word she turned and ran to the door.

"Miss Wolfe?" Nathan called out, "Miss Wolfe?" He started to follow her out the door, pulling it shut behind him. She ran down the stairs not answering him, and he caught up with her, "What's wrong? Do you need to go somewhere? I can drive you."

Angela turned to him, ashen-faced as she nodded.

"Hospital," was the only word she could manage to utter.

Nathan didn't say another word, he led her to the car and unlocked the passenger door for her, hurrying over to the other side and climbing in. They drove quietly for a few minutes until Nathan broke the silence.

"Madison Memorial?"

Angela nodded and looked out of window wordlessly.

"Miss Wolfe, is there something I can do?" He asked, after some time, glancing sideways at her as they stopped at a red light.

"Angela," she said quietly. He looked at her, confused, and she said, "Call me Angela, please."

"Um- Angela," he gulped as he spoke. "What happened? Why are we going to the hospital? I mean unless you don't want to tell me- that's alright too and-"

"It's my father." She spoke so quietly that Nathan had to make sure he hadn't misheard her.

"You father? Is he alright?"

Angela shook her head and Nathan mentally chided himself- of course her father wasn't alright, that's why he was in the hospital. He glanced again at the beautiful woman sitting next to him, and he wondered about her. He had assumed she was wealthy by the pearls around her neck and her general air, but then he had seen her apartment and reconsidered his first judgment. Now, he was itching to know more about this mysterious woman and the strange double life she seemed to lead. He was panicking because he felt that he ought to do something to help her, but he didn't know what.

"Angela?" He said after some time, as they were pulling into the hospital's driveway. "We're here."

"Right. Well, thank you," she said absent mindedly as she sat up as though he had woken her from a dream.She pushed open the car door and left without even closing it. Nathan leaned toward and pulled it shut and then parked the car before he got out. Angela had disappeared but he walked into the building and headed for the reception desk.An impatient woman glared at him.and he said,

"Um- I'm here to see Mr. Wolfe?" he said.

She scanned the list in front of her and told him a room number. He headed for the elevator and wondered whether he should be going up there.

Something kept him going, and even though he considered turning back several ties, a few minutes later he found himself standing outside a door which had "Wolfe" scrawled next to it in black marker. Taking a deep breath and squaring his shoulders, Nathan knocked on the door and waited for what seemed like an eternity for it to open. Finally, he heard footsteps approaching and he held his breath- the door was pulled open and there stood Angela with her black hair streaming down her back and shoulders, and tears clinging to her eyelashes. She blinked at him for a second, her face completely blank, and then suddenly, she threw her arms around his neck and sobbed onto his shoulder.

Chapter Six

They sat cross-legged on the rooftop of the hospital, and Angela rubbed her arms to protect herself from the chilly night air.

"Here," Nathan said, draping his jacket over her shoulders.

"No, you really don't have to-" Angela protested but Nathan shook his head and sat down.

"Thank you- for staying I mean. Daddy's surgery will take so long, and I really didn't want to be alone. But I don't know who else I could be with right now."

"It's no problem at all. I'm happy to be here," he cleared his throat and said, "If you don't mind me asking, how long has he been sick?"

Angela sighed and looked away, taking in the view from the rooftop- the stars seemed closer here, and they blinked brightly, fighting through the light pollution to shine down on her.

"If you don't want to tell me, that's alright, I respect that," Nathan said, smiling in such an easygoing manner that for a moment, Angela almost forgot her troubles, before they came crashing back and she shook her head.

"It's not that- I just don't know where to start. Well, I guess I do." She sighed and went on, "My father spent his life building an empire- he put his life and soul into his real estate business and it grew. I remember living comfortably when I was little, but as I grew up, so did our wealth. A few months ago, we were living so fabulously, it was almost sinful. But it all came to an end."

Nathan edged forward, furrowing his brows with concern.

"My father's best friend was always interested in the business, and he always said he wanted to learn so my father let him join. He made a few investments and came on the executive board. It was soon after that the accounts stopped adding up- we were losing money and nobody knew where it was going. Well, we eventually figured it out- Daddy's best friend was embezzling. But he had powerful contacts and he got out while the business crashed to the ground. The bank seized our house, and we lost everything. My father had a heart attack when he discovered that his best friend had betrayed him."

"Wow- I can't believe people do these things to their loved ones," he muttered while shaking his head.

"Well, there are some horrible people in the world. Snakes that pretend to care about you and then leave you with nothing- my father is a good person. He didn't deserve this, nobody does."

"I think you're a good person too, and I think that your father is very proud of the work that you're doing," he said nearing in.

Angela glanced up, startled.

"I know why you're so interested in restoring in that church. It's a way to salvage your father's work, and give him some peace of mind, isn't it?"

Angela nodded, and she moved closer to Nathan as well, aware of his knees touching hers now.

"I think you're a very good person, Angela."

"I think you are too- Clara told me about the program, and how it's helping you. That's admirable," she said with a warm smile.

"Maybe we can help each other," he said as he reached out to take hold of her hand.

Angela glanced at their intertwined fingers and then at him as she nodded.

"Maybe we can," before she leaned forward and gently pressed her lips against his.

They stayed like that, their cross-legged figures lit by the gentle moonlight, brought together by fate but both seeking salvation and maybe finding it in each other.

DON'T CRY, CAROLYN

MONICA MARKS

The bell was chiming again, wearing on Carolyn's already frazzled nerves. Now what does he want? I was just there! Carolyn set down her book and hurried toward the back bedroom. Her father was laying in the bed as she had left him, his breaths short and raspy. She immediately checked the dialysis machine. Content it was functioning properly, she forced a smile upon her face and turned to face the gray faced man sunken into the pillows.

"Yes dad?"

"Carolyn, I need you to go into my desk in the study and get my will." She swallowed the lump in her throat.

"Dad, stop being so fatalistic," she pleaded. "You have beaten the odds before. You will do it again."

"Don't argue with me, girl. Just do what I say. It's in the top..." he trailed off and Carolyn's blue eyes widened. She rushed to his side. Exhaling slowly, she realized he was simply catching his breath.

"...top drawer," he continued as if he had not stopped. "It is the only document there. The key is in the safe. You know the combination. It's your mother's birthday." *Why would you keep that as your password after all this time?* Carolyn thought bitterly. *You don't keep any other memory of her in this house.*

She looked uncertainly at him and then toward the door as if deciding what to do.

"Go!" he urged. There was something in his tone which caused her to move. In moments, she was back, the papers in hand. Roger struggled to sit up and Carolyn rushed to assist him.

"Dad, you don't have to do this now," she implored. "Wait until you are feeling stronger."

"I won't be feeling stronger," he informed her with finality. "This is it."

Tears sprung into her eyes and Carolyn turned her head so he would not see her cry. He would be angered by her emotion. He had raised her to be strong, not show weakness.

"Carolyn! You better not be crying!" he growled. He began to cough at his strong words and she quickly shook her head.

"I'm not," she lied, willing away the water from her lids and smiling phonily. He reached out with a trembling hand and touched her arm, his weak fingers trying to squeeze her with affection but in his enfeebled condition, Carolyn could only feel cold, lifeless fingers. He is already gone, she told herself. She could not stop the tears this time and she collapsed into a puddle of misery, burying her face in the crisp white sheets. The smell of death was in them. She knew it well.

"Stop!" Roger yelled, pounding his fists against the bed. "Stop! Look at me! Look at me! Look at me!"

"Look at me!"

Carolyn's head snapped up and she stared into the fierce brown eyes of Earl Sanders. His face was twisted into a look of disgust and he glared furiously at the nurse.

"What the hell are you doing in here? You can daydream on your own time! You've got no business doing it in here!" he barked at her. Carolyn shook off the memory and strolled further into the hospital room, a grim expression on her face.

"No need for such language, Mr. Sanders. I am here to check your vitals," she replied crisply, reaching out for his wrist. The emaciated man wrenched his arm back as if she was contagious.

"I'm not a guinea pig to be poked and prodded at!" he yelled. "You were just in here an hour ago!"

"And I will continue to come in every hour, sir." Earl spat and Carolyn narrowed her eyes, biting the insides of her cheeks to keep from losing her patience. *He knows he is dying. He is still in the anger stage. You must not allow your irritation to surface.*

"Nothing has changed," Earl snapped, settling back on the mound of pillows, eyeing Carolyn from his peripheral vision. "It doesn't matter how many times you run your useless tests. I'm still going be dead this time next week."

Carolyn cringed at his ruthless words, mostly because he was not entirely exaggerating.

"Now get out of here. You're not even a doctor!"

"I am a nurse practitioner, Mr. Sanders. I am the next best thing to a doctor that you're going to see today."

"I don't want the next best thing!" he snarled, picking up his water cup and hurling at Carolyn. "I want a real doctor. Get out!"

Sighing, Carolyn retreated from the room. There was no sense in arguing with the man. He was in his final stages of renal failure. He had been on a waiting list for five years for a new kidney, promised one twice and disappointed just as many times. Since he had joined the hospice two weeks earlier, not one person had come to visit him. His own wife, Sally Anne had passed only the previous year and Earl had no children. Carolyn was no stranger to death and the emotions which is stirred within its victims. Earl was fighting the good fight and nothing Carolyn or anyone else had to say would alleviate the hardship he was enduring. As she slowly descended the stairs to the main floor of the giant Victorian mansion, she nodded absently at a co-worker ascending the winding case.

"What's wrong, Carolyn?" Andy asked as he saw her face. She shook her dark hair, not wanting her voice to betray the sadness she was feeling. Since her own father had passed two months ago, the weight of work had seemed to suffocate her. Carolyn had been a hospice nurse for fifteen years and had always believed that the dying were the most in need of her services. Her reasoning had always been that when God decided it was time to accept them into his embrace, it was her calling to make the transition as painless as possible. She worked with her patients tirelessly to provide emotional as well as medical support. Yet since Roger had been taken from her, she had been considering another area of nursing. It all seemed for nothing. *Everyone dies. What's with all the preparation?* Her father's death had left an unfillable void in her heart, one that she felt would never stop aching. She found this puzzling since her relationship with Roger had always been strained.

"Carolyn?" She gulped back the misery in her throat and smiled weakly at Andy.

"No, nothing," she told the hospice director but the expression in his eyes told her that he wasn't buying into her claims.

"Who were you just visiting?" he pressed, turning to follow her back down the stairs.

"Earl Sanders." A look of understanding crossed over Andy's intelligent face and he gently steered Carolyn down the remaining steps and into the small area the staff used as their break room. He gestured for Carolyn to sit down and she grudgingly obliged. She was not in the mood to start a conversation with anyone at that moment but Andy was the house director and her boss essentially so Carolyn didn't see much of an opportunity for argument.

"Carolyn, may we have a discussion off the record?" he asked, closing the door to ensure for privacy. She nodded but she was battling myriad sarcastic thoughts running through her head. *Is this going to be a bonding boss moment where you tell me to 'hang in there?' and that 'things will get better if you give them time?' Because I really don't want to hear it, Andy.* Carolyn had been bombarded with platitudes since Roger had died and some days, other people's empty words were worse than the pain she was experiencing from her loss.

"Carolyn, you are hands down the best nurse we have here. I would say that you are the most qualified, compassionate medical staff I have ever encountered in my thirty years working in this field." Carolyn felt her eyebrow raise in surprise. *He doesn't look old enough to have been in any field for thirty years.* She did not speak and allowed him to finish his thought.

"Since you have joined us here at Hessler House, I can say that the palliative care the patients have received has been the best it has been in the ten years since it has been established."

Carolyn sighed. Under different circumstances, she likely would have appreciated the kind words but given her present situation, she wished Andy would get to the point so she could continue making her rounds.

"Thank you," she managed to utter but her voice lacked any sincerity. Andy leaned in toward her and Carolyn was surprised at the intimate motion.

"I have seen a change in your demeanor since your father has passed, Carolyn." Ice chips materialized in her veins and she whipped her head up to stare into his intense hazel eyes. *Oh Lord, is he firing me?* Her mind began to whirl, trying to recall what mistakes she had made over the past month since returning from her bereavement leave. *What have I done? Why can't I remember? Oh, please don't fire me! This job is all I have left. If I get fired, I won't get a job anywhere. I'll be a pariah in the field!* As if sensing her concern, Andy smiled and shook his head to ease her distressed look.

"Please don't look so stricken, Carolyn. I am simply stating an observation I have made since you have returned." Carolyn's concern abruptly turned to defensiveness.

"I have been under some stress," she replied tightly and Andy nodded.

"I understand that. And I want you to know that I am here if you need someone to talk to." Carolyn blinked, surprised by the sudden offer of friendship. She peered at him, lowering her guard slightly. In two years, she had developed a relationship of politeness with Andy, saying hello in passing, sharing the occasional cup of coffee but she would not have considered him more than an acquaintance. *He has very gentle eyes. I don't think I've ever sat this close to him before. I still wouldn't have guessed him to be in his fifties.*

"Thank you," she said again, unsure of how else to respond. She felt a slow flush building in her cheeks.

"I will try to be more focussed," she mumbled but as she said the words, she wasn't certain it was the truth.

"I didn't mean to imply that you weren't doing a wonderful job, Carolyn. On the contrary. Your work is beyond reproach. I just wanted to reach out to you. You are never alone." Carolyn shifted her eyes away, suddenly very conscious of his gaze upon her face.

"Also, I wanted to discuss Earl Sanders with you," Andy continued, settling back against the worn vinyl loveseat. Carolyn couldn't help but notice that the forest green in the sofa brought out khaki flecks in Andy's eyes. She cleared her throat, embarrassed by her thoughts and nodded. She hadn't realized she had been leaning in also and immediately righted her posture.

"There's nothing much to discuss," Carolyn said dryly. "He's dying and he's afraid. It isn't anything I haven't dealt with dozens of times in the past."

"Earl Sanders is a very difficult man," Andy said slowly. "He always has been. He and my father were in World War II together."

Carolyn was stunned by the information.

"He was a remarkable soldier, has enough accolades and medals to fill a museum. My father said that Earl once saved him from a certain prisoner of war situation by executing a daring rescue mission." Carolyn thought of the fragile old man laying in the bed upstairs and tried to envision him laying in a muddy, dangerous trench on Nazi territory. It hardly seemed fathomable but Carolyn did not doubt Andy's recount.

"He and my father remained friends throughout the war and when they got home, they both married and stayed in contact. Earl was a regular figure at our Sunday dinners and between him and my old man, they would regale us with wartime stories until our ears bled. But I think the war changed him. My father said that when they returned home, Earl was moody, sullen not at all like the jovial, happy-go-lucky man he had bonded with during the war."

Andy went silent for a moment and Carolyn cocked her head to the side.

"Why are you telling me this?" she asked finally. Andy chuckled softly.

"Maybe because I am a sentimental fool but the man upstairs is suffering inside and he needs to come to peace with whatever it is which is plaguing him before meeting our maker." The nurse began to nod slowly. *He is a man in pain, just as I am in pain.*

"I hope he will find the peace he is seeking," she told Andy earnestly.

"I think he will...provided you don't give up on him."

Carolyn rose to her feet, her mind processing what Andy had told her.

"Thank you, Andy," she told him, turning to leave.

"No, thank you, Carolyn. For everything you do."

As she left the break room, Carolyn realized she felt somewhat happy for the first time since her father had passed.

"Is he out there?"

Her dance instructor pulled the curtains aside and peered into the audience. Slowly, she withdrew her head and shook her blonde hair, a look of sympathy on her face.

"Not yet, Carolyn but I'm sure he'll be here soon," Miss Angie said with forced cheer. Disappointment flowed through her tiny frame with such force, Carolyn was afraid her knees would give way. Miss Angie was at her side, hugging her.

"He'll be here, Carolyn. Don't worry."

Sixteen-year-old Carolyn blinked quickly so her teacher would not see her expression. Her father had missed every recital that year. He would not be there. He never was. The music cued and Carolyn swallowed her bitter thoughts as she readied herself to enter the stage. Mom never missed any of my recitals. It's no wonder she left him. He was probably just as bad a husband as he is a father.

Earl Sanders was sound asleep in room 203 when Carolyn began her shift the following morning. It was barely the crack of dawn and she moved extra cautiously as to not disturb the man. Sleep was an elusive quality which had escaped Earl in the past months as he fought for his life. Despite his massive supply of pain medication, designed to lessen the symptoms of his debilitating illness, his insomnia would not ease. It was rare to see him in such as peaceful state and Carolyn had to watch him for a full minute to ensure that he was still breathing. Quietly, she paused by the wooden nightstand and lay several books at his side. She had wanted to be there to hand them to Earl personally but she dared not upset his slumber. *He will see these when he wakes. It will keep him entertained for a while.* On her tip toes, Carolyn turned to leave, smiling softly to herself. Suddenly Earl's voice rang out like a shot in a field.

"What did I tell you about coming in here, Nurse Wishes-She-Was-A-Doctor?"

Startled, Carolyn whipped around to face him.

"Oh, I'm sorry, Mr. Sanders, I didn't – "

"I didn't ask you for an apology! I asked you what you're doing in here!" Without speaking, Carolyn pointed at the bedside table, her eyes beseeching him to look. His inky eyes took on a look of stone and he peered at where her hand was pointed. If possible, his already wan face went more ashen.

"Where did you get those?" he demanded, fighting to sit up. Carolyn hurried over to assist him, concerned about his strength.

"I went online and did some research. It turns out you're a hero, Mr. Sanders," she fibbed as she adjusted his mound of pillows. He swatted her away as if she was a pesky gnat and reached for the books she had placed upon the platform.

"Have you got a hearing problem or something? I didn't ask you about me. I asked you where you got those books!"

"I bought them last night after I left here. I looked you up online and then there was a link to a Barnes and Noble directory where I could find you in print. It shows all of the battles you were in and – "

"I know what it shows!" To Carolyn's shock, Earl drew up one weak arm and feebly swiped at the pile of books, sending them flying to the floor. Carolyn reeled back, her hand flying to her mouth to hide a gasp.

"If I see you in here again, next time I won't be so nice!" Earl screamed, his face a mask of rage. Carolyn fled the room, sobs shaking her body as she flew down the winding staircase and out the door. In the sanctuary of her car she began to bawl, full body heaves of woe. *He's a monster. I don't care if he's dying. Who can treat other people like this?* She willed herself to take deep breaths and steady her shuddering body. *Dad. Dad treated people like this.*

"Carolyn, sit down." She walked into the living room, her knapsack still perched upon her slim shoulders. She adjusted her owl-like glasses and stared at her father. He was staring out the bay window in the living room.

"Can I just put my book bag upstairs?" she asked, worried that she was facing a punishment.

"No. Leave you bookbag. Sit down. I need to talk to you about something."

Very slowly, the seven-year-old ventured toward her intimidating father, lowering her pack to the floor.

"Don't leave it on the floor!" he snapped, turning away from his reverie. "Put it by the stairs."

Obediently, young Carolyn rushed to drop the bag on the steps to the backsplit and returned to where her father was pacing the floor.

"Your mother is gone," he said without preamble. Carolyn blinked uncomprehendingly at the stranger she called "dad."

"Gone where?" she questioned innocently. "To the store?"

"Don't ask stupid questions, Carolyn. I wouldn't be having a serious discussion with you if your mother had simply gone to the store, now would I?"

The child did not reply, her mind racing.

"Where did she go?" Carolyn asked meekly but she was terrified of the answer to come.

"I don't know. She left a note saying she wasn't coming back."

Tears slipped down the young girl's face and she stared up at her father.

"But why, dad? Why would she leave me?"

Roger shrugged and stopped pacing to regard his only daughter.

"Your mother has a lot of problems," he told her. "Stop crying. It won't bring her back."

Carolyn tried to wipe the streaks from her face but the tears continued to flow. Her father was growing angry.

"Stop it right now, Carolyn! You must not cry. You must be strong and always put on a brave face no matter how badly you feel inside. Do you understand?"

"Yes dad," she whispered but she didn't understand. She couldn't comprehend how her free-spirited, loving, fun mother would leave her alone with her rigid, overbearing father. She will be back for me, Carolyn told herself. She loves me. She would never leave me here with him forever.

But the days turned to weeks and the weeks, years. Madeline never returned nor did she ever contact her daughter. Carolyn was finally forced to accept that Madeline had left, tired of being suffocated by her husband and Carolyn could not blame her mother. She was tired of him too.

He is just like dad, Carolyn thought. She had finally collected herself and returned to the Hessler House. Inside one of the many bathrooms, she splashed cold water on her face and studied her reflection in the mirror. She saw so much of her father in her face and so little of Madeline. She no longer wore the huge eyeglasses, swapping them in for contact lenses as to not detract from her long lashed blue eyes. She had a mop of Roger's unruly chestnut hair and his skinny build. *I wish I had something of mom's,* Carolyn thought wistfully but was immediately ashamed by the thought. It was a rote idea, missing her mother. As the years passed, it had become harder and harder to remember what her mother looked like. Roger had either thrown out all her pictures or stored them somewhere that Carolyn would never locate them. Some nights, when Carolyn could not sleep, she would lay in bed trying desperately to hear her mother's voice saying something, anything to her but as time elapsed, Madeline's voice was as much a memory as her mother. Sighing, Carolyn redid the messy ponytail in her hair and exited the bathroom before she could acknowledge it looked worse than before. She decided to stay on the main floor for the remainder of her shift. She would have someone else tend to Earl Sanders. She was much too fragile to endure any more abuse from the man and she was just as concerned about his safety as she was about hers. With an hour left in her shift, a code blue came in on the second floor. Ginger Bellamy had passed away in room 201 and Carolyn was required to attend as the other hospice nurse was otherwise indisposed. The doctor quietly declared the death and Carolyn prepared Mrs. Bellamy for the arrival of the medical examiner. As Carolyn walked down the hall, she was intuitively aware she was about to pass Earl's room. She stepped up her gait when he called out to her.

"Hey! Nurse Next-Best-Thing-To-A-Doctor!" Carolyn was tempted to continue walking but there was something in his tone which suggested he was not on a tirade so she reluctantly stopped in the doorway. To her surprise, Earl was sitting up in bed, pouring through the books she had purchased on World War II. He waved a bony hand for her to enter but Carolyn remained in the doorway.

"Yes, Mr. Sanders?" she asked.

"Come in here a second. I want show you something in these books you bought for me," he replied, barely glancing up from his reading. Warily, Carolyn crossed the threshold toward him, prepared to run at the first hint of trouble.

"Have you got superhuman vision or something?" Earl barked. "You can't see anything from over there. Come closer."

Uncertainly, Carolyn glanced at the empty hall and then back at her patient. He did not seem threatening at that moment and it was her job to attend to him. On the contrary, in fact. He seemed to have lost twenty years off his appearance and he was smiling wistfully as if the books had put him into some sort of nostalgic time warp. Carolyn approached cautiously and glanced down where he was pointing. A glossy black and white picture of an army brigade smiled at her.

"That's me and my squad," he told her. "May of '42."

Carolyn drew in closer and peered at the photo more intently. Squinting, she could make out a very handsome Earl Sanders in a pair of army fatigues and white undershirt, a cigarette hanging out of his mouth. He looked carefree despite of his dire circumstances, grinning a charming, boyish smile. His arm was around another man who looked remarkably like Andy, the house director. As if reading her thoughts, Earl piped up.

"That snot nose brat who runs this joint? What's his name? Alfie? That's his papa, JonJon. Well, we used ta call him JonJon. His name is Jon." Carolyn found herself laughing, her initial nervousness slipping away.

"His name is Andy," Carolyn giggled but she seized the opportunity to keep him talking. "You still keep in touch with your army friends, Mr. Sanders?"

His head whipped up at her and he scowled.

"If you're going to poke and prod at me all day like some hamster in a cage, you can probably call me Earl," he snapped. "And aside from Jonny, no, they're all dead now. Or have dementia so no point in bugging them to discuss old times."

Carolyn thought she felt her heart break slightly. *No wonder he's so miserable. He has no one. He's going to die alone. Just like dad did.*

"Don't look at me with pity eyes, nursey. I had a good life," Earl told her, noticing the shadow which crossed over her blue irises.

"I'm sure you did, Earl. From what I can see, you've lived five lives. But surely there must be someone you want here with you, you know, someone to hold your hand..." Carolyn trailed off, suddenly embarrassed under his scrutinizing stare.

"For when I kick the bucket?" Carolyn grimaced at the word choice and glanced down at her white shoes.

To her surprise, he began to laugh.

"The only person I want with me has been gone for a long while," he told her, closing the book and sitting back. Carolyn wanted to kick herself for her insensitive comment. *The man just lost his wife. Good work reminding him of that in his darkest hour.*

"I'm sorry about your wife," she whispered, hanging her head. Again, Earl chortled and Carolyn stared at him, appalled by his reaction.

"Nah, I didn't mean Sally Anne, God rest her beautiful soul. But Sally Anne wasn't the love of my life." Carolyn found herself sitting, enthralled by Earl's brutally honest words. It was not surprising that he was pouring his heart out to her as near the end, patients often felt the need to unleash the burdens they kept deep in their soul but Carolyn was startled all the same.

"Who was the love of your life?" she pressed.

"Her name was Glenda Thompson and she was my entire world." Earl's face softened as he tried to recall the delicate features of the woman once he had obviously cared for very deeply. "She and I were joined at the hip from dawn until dusk every day since we were knee high to grasshoppers. We sat together in class, walked home from school together. She loved me more than anyone ever had before or did again."

"What happened to her, Earl?"

"I happened to her. While I wasn't old enough to be drafted, I wanted to serve my country but most of all, I was eighteen and scared. Maybe I thought I was too young to be tied down to one woman.

Hindsight is always twenty-twenty, isn't it? I ran off to join the army and slunk off like a thief in the night without saying good-bye."

"Why?" Carolyn was aghast. "I thought she was the love of your life!"

Earl shrugged.

"Weren't you ever eighteen and scared? I was stupid. I spent my entire tour pining for her but I didn't write her once. I was a kid with stupid kid emotions and stupid kid thoughts. I thought when I get home, she'll still be there, waiting for me."

"She wasn't, was she?"

Earl shook his head and for a moment, Carolyn thought she saw tears mist his eyes.

"Nope. Married Jerry Malcom. That blockhead was the dumbest kid in our class. I swear she did it out of spite. We never spoke again but I'll tell you, Nurse, I have never stopped thinking about the way that woman made me feel. I loved Sally Anne, truly I do but she never made my heart race like Glenda did. I was happy with my wife but I always wondered what became of Glenda Thompson." Earl's eyelids were getting heavy and Carolyn rose to her feet slowly.

"Get some rest, Earl. I'll be back tomorrow and you can tell me some more war stories, okay?"

"Hey, nursey," he called sluggishly. Carolyn turned to regard him.

"Yes Earl?"

"I'm sorry I was being such a jerk to you. It's just..."

"I know, Earl. No need to apologize. See you tomorrow, okay?" He was already falling asleep and Carolyn backed out of the room as he nodded slightly, acknowledging her words. Carolyn hurried toward Andy's office. *I must find Glenda Thompson before it's too late.*

She glanced up at the address again to confirm and then put the car in park. *This is a really bad idea,* she repeated to herself as she made her way up to the apartment building. *But Earl deserves some peace on his deathbed. You have to at least try to do this for Earl.* Inside, she stared at the names on the intercom. She jabbed at a button and waited, resisting the urge to run away and abort the mission altogether. Before she could do the sensible thing and leave, a woman's voice piped through the voice box.

"Yes?"

"Mrs. Malcom?"

A slight pause followed the question.

"Yes. Who is this?"

"My name is Carolyn Ward. I am a hospice nurse at Hessler House in Lafayette. Do you think we could speak for a moment?"

Instantly, the door buzzed to allow for Carolyn to enter and she ran up the third-floor walk-up to Glenda Malcom's apartment. Glenda was already standing in the hall in wait, a handsome older woman in her late eighties. As Carolyn searched her face, she could see how Earl would have been so smitten with her in his youth. She was a stunning combination of elegance and fire. She peered at Carolyn curiously before ushering her into her tiny dwelling.

"Welcome to my humble abode," Glenda said wryly, gesturing about the bachelor apartment.

"Do you live here alone?" Carolyn asked once they had been seated at the small kitchen table which doubled as a coffee and sofa table.

"Since my divorce twenty years ago, yes," Glenda conceded. "Don't need much more than this at my age."

"You're divorced from Jerry Malcom?" Carolyn could hardly believe what she was hearing. Glenda's eyes narrowed at the sound of her ex-husband's name.

"Yes. I'm sorry, what are you doing here?" she demanded, her tone slightly frosty.

"I am a nurse at Hessler House. It is a hospice in Lafayette. One of my patients used to be...acquainted with you," Carolyn faltered. Glenda Malcom sat back, a suspicious expression in her face.

"If this is some kind of catfish scam, lady, you can't take me for anything," she snapped and Carolyn almost laughed. "My grandkids have me wired on the interweb and I haven't got a nickel to part with."

"No, ma'am. My patient's name is Earl Sanders. Do you remember him?"

As if a light had been switched on in her face, Glenda's expression exploded into excitement.

"Early? You know Early?" she cried, leaning forward to grasp Carolyn's hands. The nurse nodded and then watched as the happiness drained from her face.

"Wait, didn't you say you're from a hospice? He's dying?" she whispered and Carolyn bobbed her head again, hanging her head.

"I was hoping you would come with me back to the house so he can see you one last time. I fear you are his one who got away," Carolyn told her gently and Glenda nodded immediately rising to her feet.

"Although God knows he doesn't deserve it, leaving me all those millions of years ago!"

"He has regretted it every day for seventy years, Glenda."

"He better have!" she shouted, locking the door and hurrying after Carolyn.

Earl was asleep when Carolyn brought Glenda to the hospice. It was early evening and as they approached his bed, there was something about his expression which instantly alarmed Carolyn. She pressed the call button by his bed.

"What's wrong?" Glenda screeched. "Is he dead?"

"No, no, Mrs. Malcom. He's alive," Carolyn assured her but her heart was racing as she recognized something in Earl's serene face. The night nurse arrived.

"Has he passed, Carolyn?" Sandra asked, rushing toward Earl but Carolyn shook her head.

"No, Sandy. Why is he still sleeping?" she asked but in her heart, she already knew the answer. Sandra blinked and stared at Carolyn.

"He has been sedated because of his agitation. The delirium hasn't set in from pain so we had to put him under."

"Under?" Glenda yelled. "What do you mean? Wake him up! I want to talk to him and tell him how much I have missed him all of these years! I want him to know that I married the wrong man and I should have waited for him! I want him to know I've always loved him!"

Carolyn swallowed the lump in her throat and shook her head miserably. She had been too late.

"It's too late," she whispered. "He is in a coma and will remain in one until he passes. It is the most painless way for him to go."

Glenda let out an anguished cry, a feral, penetrating sound which pierced the hearts of everyone in earshot.

"No! Earl, I'm sorry! I've always loved you! Early, wake up, please!"

Carolyn put her hand gently on Glenda's shoulder as her face fell into the sheets. The old woman grasped his hand tightly.

"He knows," Carolyn whispered. "He has always known."

"Stop your crying, Carolyn, stop it!"

"Dad, I can't! You're dying and I can't watch this!"

She turned and ran from the house, leaving the door wide open in her wake. She could not watch him suffering, could not handle the thought of tending to his corpse. She collapsed on the front lawn and curled into a ball. Mom, why did you leave us? I need you to help me through this? How could you leave me alone with him for all of this time? I can't do this! Carolyn sat up suddenly, realizing what she had done and scrambled back into the house. Roger lay in his bed, his eyes open in a perpetual stare of eternal sleep, clutching a letter in his hand. Choking on her sobs, Carolyn retrieved the note and read it.

Dear Carolyn,

I know you have always thought me to be a harsh and demanding man, especially in the absence of your mother. I always tried my best to shield you from the realities of who your mother was while providing for you. I missed your childhood because I was working, endlessly working. You may not recall but I often did sixty or seventy hour weeks. Your mother accumulated a mountain of debt in our names before she disappeared with the neighbor's son. I quietly paid for the neighbor to move so that the scandal would not ever reach your ears. I lived in constant fear that you would hear about Madeline's drunken escapades with other men, some of them young enough to be her own child. I lived in constant fear that you would turn to the bottle yourself one day as you always wore the same expression of melancholy which she did. I lived in constant fear that you would abandon me, just as she did and God knows, I tried every way I knew how to ensure none of these things occurred. Yes, I was tough on you but I was tougher on myself. I have always loved you very much and perhaps I did not show it when I was alive but I hope that in my death you can understand why I did what I did.

Until the pearly gates reunite us once more,
Daddy

The sun was shining and the birds singing a squabbling song above the cemetery when Carolyn approached with the roses. Leaning over, she wiped dirt off the epitaph and lay the flowers on the grave. It was the first time she had come since his death and she didn't know what to say. Pausing, she looked to the heavens as if expecting the word of God to guide her. Suddenly a smile, a true, genuine beam lit her face as if she had an epiphany and she looked down at where her father was laying to rest.

"I forgive you, dad," she whispered, turning away. Fifty yards away, under a weeping willow tree, Andy held out his hand.

"Are you ready?" he asked. *Yes. Yes, I am ready to move on now,* she told herself. Nodding, she accepted his outstretched palm and the two headed off into the sunlight.